Storming Heaven

Storming Heaven

Roger Yates

Bloomdido Books

Contents

Chapter One

Le Moulin de la Galette

In the summer of 1870 two windmills stood on the heights of Montmartre, then an open hilltop just inside the newly-constructed bastions of Paris. The hill bore a small vineyard and an assembly of narrow fields, allotments and old sheds separated by ragged fencing. Between the two windmills, beside the road to the fields, there was an arbour of tamarisk trees with benches and tables beneath them and an area of bare earth cleared for dancing. Dances were held there throughout the summer on weekday evenings and all day on Sundays.

The place had a long history of pleasure-seeking. It was then two hundred years old and took its name from a kind of sweet pancake made with flower milled there that was enjoyed by the villagers of Montmartre over a glass of wine. Montmartre was still a village in many ways, although it had doubled its population in the previous few decades as Haussmann demolished the old rebellious quarters of Paris and built the boulevards of the City of Light. But the village girls - seamstresses, clothes-makers, flower makers and washerwomen still danced with their men under the trees.

Perhaps they attracted young men of the bohemian bourgeoisie, painters, or writers, but the place was still run for them on their terms. Montmartre had a reputation for its freedom and for a population proud to call itself *la canaille*, the mob. It had a history of resistance too. The father of the present owner had fought off the invading Cossacks of 1814 and his dismembered body was hung from the sails in reprisal.

The mill no longer ground flour. But once a year the sails were set, the wind shaft turned and the stones ground orris roots for perfume. In a house behind the mill lived an old perfumer. Above her house were two fields of irises, which were admired by Van Gough when he painted the area twenty years later. The old woman was also a midwife and housed waifs and strays for the community. She was a veteran of the revolutions of 1830 and 1848 and considered a wise woman in Montmartre. Her annual preparations made the Moulin de la Galette fragrant for months.

At the far end of the earth track that led up past the windmills and onto the flat expanse of the hill, a field housed the wagons and caravans of a circus. Fair booths, old sheds, tethered horses and piles of firewood littered the place. Circus was an industry in Montmartre. The village had been a horse fair in the middle ages. Street performance had a long history there.

One day in the mid-sixties the perfumer was brought a child. A girl of about eight years old had been discovered face down in the road with her mouth full of coal and sand. She was wearing a ragged black dress, no shoes, her dark hair unkempt. She responded to questions by singing and laughing. She also stood on her hands. The perfumer was consulted, inquiries were set in train, and Mlle Michel, the school mistress, was asked to pay a visit.

The girl answered to the name of Monelle. No trace of her origin could be found. Paris was filled with lost children. There was no authority that would take an interest. The perfumer knew the Church would step in if asked, and claim another girl to work for free to the disadvantage of other working women. The priests would love to get their hands on her. She found her a warm nook beside the perfume still, cooked a hot meal, and ignored her.

Monelle descended on the neighbourhood like a black wind. She learned to release the sails on the windmill and set the great grindstone rumbling. She fought the descending sails with a stick and was knocked over by them. She released the circus horses and rode bareback on them. She rounded up the local curs and led a pack to chase the pigs that hung around the open drains down in the village. She stole without shame.

Mlle Michel came to the house behind the windmill in the evenings and began to teach the child to read and write. The middle-aged schoolmistress was a partner in a school in lower Montmartre that made scarcely enough money to feed its teachers, who were as poor as the working-class women whose children they taught. Mlle Michel's teaching partner was said to have taught all Montmartre to read in her time and had been a comrade of the perfumer in '48.

Michel soon took Monelle up to the circus and suggested (it was really an order) that they teach the girl everything they knew. She then produced a coin and challenged the Circus Master to a shooting match. A showman's shooting booth was permanently set up nearby. She carefully selected an air rifle and won hands down. She collected nearly a franc before the old man, and others who came to try their luck, conceded defeat. This was a regular ritual. Her winnings always went into the school kitty. But she shared the few sous she had stolen from the Master's caravan with Monelle.

"I bet him with his own money!"

The wind of the Heights blew her hair and cloak back. Monelle grabbed her hand and looked up at her as an equal.

"Let's go and feed the bats," said Mlle Michel.

Louise Michel was a poet of some distinction and a long-time friend and occasional lover of Victor Hugo. She had sent verses to him as a child. When they first met she was just twenty. She was the daughter of a peasant girl of great beauty who had been brought up in the household of an impoverished aristocrat in Haute Marne. The son of the family left home soon after the girl was born, but her mother remained living nearby and retained the freedom of the house. Louise was brought up by her grandparents. She was given the family name. Her grandfather and grandmother were not in doubt about her ancestry. She had the webbed toes of the line. They were free thinking republicans with a library filled with works of the Enlightenment: Diderot, Voltaire, Rousseau, and of the modern revolutionaries Blanqui and Proudhon.

The sombre, square, fortified house looked like a tomb from the outside, but it was a place of freedom and hope within. The family horse walked through the rooms begging biscuits. Rescued cats and a small pack of dogs filled the place. Louise tamed a barn owl which lived in one of the towers that stood at each corner of the house. She loved its phosphorescent eyes. She wandered the forest nearby seeking to contact the wolves. She thought they followed her. She invoked druidic powers beside an oak tree. She tried without success to summon the devil, and her interest in religion ended there. She stole her grandfather's keys and cut a set of her own. She pilfered food and sums of money and gave them to the poor. She devised plays from the works of Victor Hugo. She sent him verses. He wrote back. In her teens she was presented to suitors. The old couple dutifully sought a husband for her. She insulted them all, on one occasion arriving wearing a short mud-splattered dress with a net full of toads in her pocket. The suitor left with her mockery in his ears and a toad in his pocket. She learned music. The family performed together while she played an ancient piano. She wrote operas.

When, in her teens, the old couple died the house was shut up and fell quickly into complete dereliction. Her mother had some land and a vineyard nearby. Michel, refusing to marry, became a school teacher. A school mistress earned less than a cook, but she was free. It was also a suitable occupation for a revolutionary. She had read Hugo, the revolutionary writings of Auguste Blanqui and the anarchist Proudhon in their entirety.

"They will like some milk," said Mlle Michel.

She disengaged her hand from the child and produced a large hunting knife from inside her cloak. She cut a straw with it which she gave to Monelle and then threw the knife with considerable force and accuracy into a fence-post.

"Ask the Master at the circus to teach you to throw knives," she said. She gave Monelle the knife to carry while she took possession of the straw.

Michel and Monelle begged a little milk from the old perfumer and then climbed the tower of the Moulin de la Galette. The teacher had noticed the bats around the lamps in the tamarisk trees over the dance floor on summer evenings, and came to find them up there. She reached up into the mechanism and caught a sleeping bat. Its wings wrapped around her hand. She gently released its grip and hung it on Monelle's dress-front. She sucked milk up in the straw and fed it in drops into the little creature's mouth.[1]

Now, in August 1870, Monelle read Hugo, Proudhon and Marx. She could stand up on a horse. She threw knives at the circus boy L'Oursin , another stray child who had run away from a building site and hung around the circus until they accepted him. She had joined the Society of Women's Rights and knew Andre Leo, the novelist and political activist who had organized it. She had read most of

Leo's books. She was a member of the International. She cultivated the appearance of an enraged waif and could still pass as a child. She was bright, angry and fearless. Under Louise Michel's tutorship she became a more dangerous monster than she had ever been. She had already spent some time in jail. She may have killed a man.

Monelle worked tirelessly. She was a street artist, and drew scandalous cartoons of Napoleon III on pavements in the city with stolen charcoal. It eventually cost her a year in prison. She sang in the street too, dressed always in red or black: shortish, flared skirts over a sturdy leotard and tights with soft acrobats' boots on her feet. She would do summersaults, cartwheels and handstands, sometimes falling into the crowd and coming out of it with a purse or a pocket book. She performed for the circus. She sang and danced with the small band at the Moulin de la Galette. She ordered performance clothes from the seamstresses of the neighbourhood who competed with one another to produce costumes for her. She soon returned the dresses to them to be unpicked and the material used to make clothes for their children. She gave the rest of her money away. All of it. If Monelle needed a sou she went down into the city and stole it. The old perfumer was soon able to enlarge her cooperative and bring more fields under iris cultivation with her help.

Like Monelle, the seamstresses who danced at the Moulin de la Galette were beautifully dressed. Dress-making was the biggest industry in the Paris of the late Empire. Building followed it a close second. There was a massive pool of recirculating clothes and materials available to a population with no spare money. The seamstresses worked from home, where costs to the proprietors were less. A huge quantity of fabric was always distributed around working class Paris. The girls dancing at the Moulin de la Galette may not quite have owned the clothes they wore, but they were mistresses of the art of preparing, cleaning and working cloth. It was not unusual to see a woman in an elegant, bustled and bowed gown with only clogs to her feet, dancing barefoot in the soft dust of the dance floor. The women who wore these dresses had designed them too. Everything rises up from the bottom.

There was a pool of musicians in Montmartre to play for dancers at the Moulin de la Galette, or to accompany the circus when the big tent went up. Something could always be arranged when both entertainments were engaged on the same night. But Monelle's first duty was always to the circus band in which her friend L'Oursin also played.

L'Oursin had graduated from a den in the circus woodpile to a comfortable shed with a small wood-burning stove in it, and from rags to a kind of black and red bandsman's uniform. It had been discovered that he could play any musical instrument. He played a leaky clarinet with ease. The Master was so impressed he dug out an old saxophone and had the circus mechanic repair it. L'Oursin was sent to Mlle Michel, who taught him to read music in the school. She made him learn to read French at the same time. Michel was working sixteen hours a day.

When the circus was resting Monelle and L'Orsin played for the dancers. The band comprised a tuba, trombone, trumpet and percussion. Sometimes clarinettists or string players enlarged it. Monelle sang in a voice and style that would be echoed by Edith Piaf seventy years later. She sang the most popular love song of the time *Le Temps des Cerise,* "In Cherry Blossom Time."

"In cherry blossom time

When the gay nightingale and mocking blackbird sing

Lovers will have the sun in their hearts."

The band executed a brisk, military waltz accompaniment that made the song sound like a call to arms. Late on summer evenings she sang it quietly for the lovers, accompanying herself on a guitar while L'Oursin collected glasses and finished off the dregs. The summer seemed endless to the two children on the edge of the adult world. Monelle and L'Oursin were fierce with life. They had both emerged from experiences that they never talked about. Rather they converted their anger and grief into action, performance and criminality with a kind of joyful rage that was never very far from actual violence.

All Montmartre seemed to pass by the Moulin de la Galette on a sunny Sunday. Louise Michel, if she was not working, would pause on the road to enjoy the music before visiting her old friend the perfumer. When the lights in the tamarisk trees were lit, Monelle and L'Oursin would sometimes clear the dance floor by dancing a display cancan together. This was not the chorus-line dance which was a confection of later variety theatres, but a working class dance danced by couples, the men, too, high kicking. L'Oursin and Monelle turned somersaults and cartwheels. He threw her around. The performance ended with them singing parts in a bawdy song mocking a lover's tiff, or she sang from the bandstand in a flame red dress, her face made up white and red, her lips a perfect cupid's bow, her black hair shining in the stage lights that could give her face a ghastly hollow quality, a demonic dance-macabre impression that she surely cultivated.

Monelle's stage persona was perhaps a fitting symbol for working class Paris of the late Empire. She represented the poor of the city as the half-starved victim of its decadence, coming out of the limelight at her audience like a demonic force, unbowed, celebratory and dangerous. Immense political and economic forces had been grinding over Paris during the previous decades. Much of the old working class centre of the city had been rebuilt and its population driven into newly annexed outlying districts. An arc of poverty enclosed the city from the north in les Batignoles, Montmartre and Belleville. In the centre the new boulevards shone with a kind of bland novelty, their perspectives converging on nothing. New palaces, scaffolding, blocks of stone, piles of rafters, of rough-hewn cornices, the huge stone blocks stained green in puddles of water had risen, conjured into being by an army of ragged men, Babylon King's men working a vast building site stretching up towards the sun, panelling fine ceilings under false skies, workers who would soon be removed from the scene, like the rubbish left behind by the construction work. Louis Napoleon, that gold-braided popinjay surrounded by a circle of arrogant courtiers, presided over a massive accumulation of capital into the hands of the bourgeoisie. Huge debts were owed by the state for the Haussmann reconstruction. The Church and the army thrived. Generals flattered him. A challenge to Bismarck and the emerged state of Prussia had been recommended to placate a population always divided by the demand for a Republic. The French army was hailed as the greatest military force on earth. The Emperor believed his inheritance from Bonaparte made him militarily invincible. Many of the workers who had built Haussmann's city flowed into the army to escape unemployment and feed families crowded into the outlying slums. Since July the country had been on a war footing.

But the Heights of Montmartre on a sunny Sunday seemed a long way away from the folly and arrogance of Power. After working all week far into the nights in the crowded streets below, the women and girls from the clothing industry, who had no families to support, came up to the Moulin de la Galette to dance. Their fingers were swollen and painful with needle pricks and thread cuts. Perhaps they smelled a little of the petrol-based dry cleaning liquids, newly pioneered in Paris, that they had used to freshen up the dresses they wore, masked by the scent sold to them at little above cost by the old perfumer, but the girls shone with youth. The lambent air of the heights softened both colour and outline with its vaguely milky quality, a soft haze that warmed skin tones and made fabrics glow. Under the tamarisk trees the dappled light was pink and violet. The tall glasses and carafes on the tables glinted like ice. The white lighting globes in the trees looked as delicate as frozen bubbles. Young men in straw hats, their faces flushed with wine and youth, gazed in amorous reverie at the girls who wore the bustled and ruched floor-length gowns of the era, but in light colours, not the dark of bourgeois street dress, pinks and blues with big decorative bows. The music and the conversation invigorated everything, seemed to make the dapples of pinkish sunlight on the dark jackets of the men swirl and dance.

Monelle and L'Orsin led the band on those occasions they were present. The musical education Mlle Michel had given them enabled them to write parts and copy the sheet music stolen from the music shops down in Paris by Monelle. Music at the Moulin de la Galette was always abreast of the latest fashion. And she sang! Sometimes she extemporized political themes:

"In cherry blossom time,

When the red flags fly

And the mocking blackbird."

She sang verses mocking Louis Napoleon, calling for a Republic, which were woven ironically and on the spot into popular chansons. The band, prompted by L'Oursin, might suddenly insert a quote from the Marseillaise, always a revolutionary song for the poor, to cheers from the dancers. She sang of love and revolution as if they were the same thing. She sang in the harsh argot of the streets, and, slightly ironically, but touching the heart too, in the fulsome, high-romantic style of popular song. She was irresistible when she sang.

Mlle Michel did not dance, and she wore black, but there any similarity with a bourgeois spinster school mistress ended. She never wore a hat or bonnet in an era when it was always considered disreputable, even shameful for a woman to be bare-headed in public. Her thick shoulder-length hair was often unkempt and never coifed up or braided. She frequently wore a man's cloak over a dark dress twenty years out of date and without the ridiculous bustle and elaboration of the present fashion. She attended the funeral of the republican journalist Victor Noir, shot by the nephew of Louis Napoleon, Pierre Bonaparte in a dual, dressed as a man and carrying her uncle's sabre, fully expecting to see the start of a revolution. It was a surprise to everyone that the event passed off without bloodshed. A hundred thousand people, republican and revolutionary, followed the coffin and overcame an attempt by the army to stop them. Red flags flew on the road to Neuilly where a few months later Louise Michel was to see fierce fighting.

Michel had grown into middle age teaching the poor of Montmartre and attending educational lectures herself. She was of that generation of women who were fighting for educational equality with men in a decade of revolutionary upheaval across Europe. Russian women, like Elizabeth Dmitrieff who had been drawn into the political vortex of Paris, had to travel to Switzerland for an education. In Russia the Czar was ruthlessly repressing Nihilists who's "no" opposed the old power structures. Education for women was out of the question. In France the first woman to attain a Baccalaureate had been refused the certificate. But lectures by radicals on new ideas were being attended by tens of thousands of people in the Paris of the late sixties. These were people of the small bourgeoisie, printers, tradesmen and women, skilled artisans as well as the dispossessed. Revolution seemed inevitable in those years. Michel attended the lectures of Louis Auguste Blanqui, a romantic revolutionary socialist already active for thirty years who proposed the overthrow of the bourgeoisie for its own sake and the dictatorship of a heroic revolutionary elite. She was to become close friends with two of his followers, Raoul Rigault, later chief of police for the Commune and his assistant Théophilé Ferre. She taught in adult education herself, in a school also taught by Charles de Sivry, who was to become Paul Verlaine's brother in law and to save the manuscripts of Rimbaud's "A Season in Hell" and "Illuminations" from destruction. She corresponded with Victor Hugo in exile in Brussels. And she wrote. She thought of herself first as a poet. Her output was enormous. She sent a book's length series of insulting satirical verses to the Emperor over the years and kept no copies. She published under the male name Enjolras, a pet name that Hugo had given her. She left manuscripts to be ignored by publishers, and forgot about them, or was too proud to ask for them back. She wrote music too, composing operas of wild dissonance scored for an orchestra that included cannon. She cared nothing that they would never be performed and refused to waste time seeking a publisher. She was too busy for self-promotion.

To be a poet was a greater task than producing manuscripts. It was a heroic role. Hugo was her mentor. She called him "Master" in her letters. And it was as a poet of the real that she was to surpass him.

The circus loaded up its waggons and showman's caravans and descended from the Heights of Montmartre into the squares and parks of Paris a few times each summer. It also toured the near villages and towns. Descended is perhaps an apt word: the tours were an undertaking of military complexity intent on pillage. Putting up the tent was itself a military operation. It was taboo for any part canvass to touch the ground. The huge squares that made up the canopy lay rolled up and folded on four wagons. After the masts had been raised and made secure, the sheeting was unwound from the carts and carried in the arms of a line of men who slowly unrolled the bulky material as it was hauled up. A gust of wind catching a sail area of that size would throw anyone attempting to hold it down right over the masts with ease. L'Oursin and the other tumblers deftly hitched mooring ropes to the long iron tent pegs driven into the ground to prevent that happening.

The seamstresses of Montmartre made the circus clothes, and at least one dressmaker from the neighbourhood always travelled with them. Monelle stood on her horse dressed like a ballerina in a cloud of insubstantial white material, white tights, and gold slippers. A steam-powered electrical generator fed the lights. Electricity was still a rarity first seen at the Great Exhibition only a few years previously. This was not a large circus, with only modest high-wire acts and no exotic animals, but the costumes, the lighting and the colour made it distinct. Monelle put the dogs through their act wearing fantastic, baggy pantaloons ruffed at the ankles, with yellow bows in her hair and a short blue velvet tailed coat. She looked like one of her poodles. The costumes were always on the edge of the surreal, the make-up, with sharply outlined, prim lips and white skin, discreetly alarming. She played Columbine to L'Oursin's Harlequin and the Master's Pierrot and enhanced the role with a shadow of the macabre. L'Oursin wore a yellow and green diamond patterned costume. The Master looked like death.

On those summer nights in the Champ de Mars where the Great Exhibition had been held three years previously and where the circus had pitched up, Paris seemed unassailable. It was the holy city established in the West. A wild rumour circulated that the Prussians had been defeated. People embraced in the street. In the circus the clowns chased Otto von Bismarck around the ring with explosions and alarms. But the rumour turned out to have originated in the Stock Exchange where small fortunes were made as a result. No one seemed very concerned that Prussian forces were on French soil. Monelle cared not at all. Her opinions about wars between bourgeois states had been formed in meetings of the International. She differed sharply with Mlle Michel about how sacred the soil of Alsace was and told her so. She taught revolution to her fellow artists. The Master was a republican with memories of both '30 and '48. He said nothing. He had seen fighting at barricades before. And he respected her. The savage waif that he had inherited from Mlle Michel was one of the finest performers he had ever known. He loved her like a daughter. In any case the circus was the only reality he acknowledged. Creating a pool of light and colour in which to play Pierrot was his sole passion.

Now, in late August, the circus was back in its own field above the windmills. L'Oursin and Monelle hung around the Moulin de la Galette but money was scarce that year. So they went busking and thieving along the new boulevards. One Sunday at the end of the month Monelle went up to the circus field to find L'Oursin. He was writing parts in his little shed.

"Let's do the cemetery caper today," she said at the door.

"You're too old now!"

"You'll see."

She ran down into the twisting lanes of Montmartre and called in to see one of the circus seamstresses. She returned looking like an eight year old in mourning. They ran, looking quite incongruous, he in working clothes running with the curious noisy shuffling gait of one wearing clogs, and she veiled and in black, all the way to the great necropolis at Pere Lachaise. There she found a fresh grave, and while he kept a watch over her from among the tombs she threw herself on the flowers sobbing inconsolably. Before long a little crowd had gathered.

"Oh I am too unhappy!"

Between terrible bouts of weeping she revealed that she was now a penniless orphan nearly dead from hunger. She had come to die on her mother's grave. Before long francs were being placed on a handkerchief laid on the grave beside her. Gentlemen in top hats gently ushered their wives from the scene. She made twenty francs in under an hour, and when L'Oursin whistled a warning that cemetery officials were approaching she ran like the wind.

L'Oursin caught up with her on the way back to Montmartre. She gave ten francs to a soldier amputee begging on the street and directed him to *La Marmite,* a cooperative café run by the anarchist labour activist Natalie Lemel. She gave five francs to the seamstress who had lent her the clothes. She split the remaining five francs with L'Oursin. In the Moulin de la Galette they bought two glasses of green absinthe.

A hundred miles to the east tens of thousands of young men were moving slowly into battle. Prussian forces had already left thousands of dead French youths and men on battlefields further south. In a stuffy provincial town not far from the place where the Emperor himself commanded the best of the French army a young poet in his school holiday was selling his books. In Charleville, in the Ardennes hills not far from the Belgian border Arthur Rimbaud, fifteen, was planning to run away from home to Paris.

Chapter Two

Blackcurrant River

Nothing in Charleville suggested that two great armies were preparing for battle nearby. The band on the decorative bandstand in Station Square played for the Sunday strollers around the tailored gardens with their "Keep off the Grass" notices on the lawns. The gentry of the town sweated in the late summer heat under their finest top hats and broadcloth their bustled wives shaded by parasols. A group of well-dressed young men in dandyish clothes and straw boaters observed the girls. Four fat burghers sat in a row on a bench with cerise faces, poking the ground with their sticks, breathing heavily and mumbling in their padded, gold watch-chained guts. The Emperor was at the helm. The army was ready down to the last white gaiter button. Splendid chaps! Bismarck was soon sure to sue for peace. Suddenly an overgrown child with scruffy hair wearing a long grubby overcoat despite the heat and smoking a pipe clenched between his teeth crossed the square from the side shaded by big horse chestnut trees where he had been glaring with an attitude of concentrated lust at some girls. He had a dozen books under each arm. His worn-down boots were not laced up. He walked right across the lawns and through a bed of peonies. He barged between the young dandies forcing them to move out of his way.

"Well really! Good Lord. Watch out!"

Before the full impudence of his actions had sunk in Rimbaud was across the square and round the corner.

Because it was Sunday he banged on the back door of the bookshop. When the bookseller eventually opened up he walked in uninvited and piled the books on the kitchen table where a stack of them slowly toppled onto a plate of cakes. He pointed at bookseller's startled wife.

"Who's that?"

The bookseller was in his shirt-sleeves scratching at the scant hair he combed over his bald spot. Rimbaud spread the books out, pushing back some coffee cups and handed the plate of squashed cakes to the wife to clear out of his way.

"The new Mallarme is hardly touched. Three francs. This Banville is so flowery you could put it on a fucking grave. Three francs." He scooped up some cream from the book with his forefinger and stuck it in his mouth, slowly withdrawing it from lips as fresh as a girl's.

The bookseller flinched. His wife said,

"Will you taste some coffee Monsieur?"

"All right. Why not. Whatever you like," replied Arthur Rimbaud. He sat down and lit his pipe.

The bookseller, in agony to see the back of this disgusting youth, agreed to everything. He eventually went to fetch the money. But Arthur had grown attached to his chair. He knocked the dottle out of his pipe into his coffee cup. He took a pipe-cleaner from his pocket and started to clean it. He was discoursing on the ithyphallic in Greek art with explicit hand gestures. He held the pipe-cleaner, freshly withdrawn from the pipe, delicately between his fingers. He put it down and looked up at the horrified couple. It left a long brown stain on the table-cloth.

At the station Rimbaud discovered that the Prussian army had inconveniently cut the line from Charleville to Paris so he bought a ticket to Charleroi in Belgium. There he had to change his money into Belgian francs at a bad exchange rate in order to buy a ticket for a rout open into the north of Paris. His money didn't stretch now to a ticket all the way. He hid under a seat. At Gare du Nord, walking nonchalantly along with his pipe in his jaw and the collar of his overcoat turned up, he was intercepted by a ticket inspector.

"Ticket?"

Rimbaud became aggressive immediately.

"My good man! I am late for an appointment to meet the poet Verlaine."

The ticket inspector seized his arm. Another appeared and they marched him into an office. Arthur rummaged through his pockets as if he expected to discover the ticket at any moment. He produced a horrible, stiff, yellowing handkerchief a handful of shag tobacco, a few Belgian coins, a chewed pencil and a notebook filled with incomprehensible writings. He dumped the lot on the inspector's desk.

"Age?"

"I am seventeen and a half."

"Address?"

Rimbaud kept quiet.

In the police holding pens across the city he was shoved into a crowded and stinking courtyard. Before he knew it the tobacco and pipe had been removed from his pockets, the notebook thrown into the pissed-up corner of the yard and someone had given him a kiss, to laughter and shouts of approval. He kicked around him with his heavy boots and was left alone from then on. The magistrate looked with mild interest when the curious urchin before him quoted Plato on imprisonment in Greek. He sent him to Mazas prison on charges of theft and vagrancy. Had Rimbaud not lied about his age and given his address he would have been set free.

Mazas Prison was a panopticon, a modern, circular design based on the humane principles of Jeremy Bentham. After his head had been shaved and he had been drenched in disinfectant he was brought before the governor. It was explained to him what a panopticon was, that the prison was a building designed so that he would be under continual surveillance for his own moral improvement.

"I know what panopticon means," said Arthur Rimbaud, giving the governor an icy stare. "I am a poet, sir. A poet *is* Argus Panoptes who guards the world with his thousand eyes. I will be keeping my eyes on you."

His feet touched the ground in a narrow cell, a thin wedge-shaped slice of the building with a window high up in the curved outer wall and a door at the narrow end. It held a table, a chair, a hammock and a toilet that reeked of disinfectant, something more or less unknown in that era. Not far away was another prisoner, Émile Eudes, a friend of Victor Hugo and the husband of Louise Michel's close friend Victorine. Eudes had been sentenced to death a few days earlier for attempting to incite a republican uprising.

He was in prison for a week and at first he liked it well enough. It was a dramatic and poetic interlude that would impress his friends. It was also the first time he had ever been alone and the first time nothing was expected of him. When his clothes were returned, stinking of fumigant, he found the pencil and the notebook were in a pocket. He marked off the days on the wall and started a poem, "The dead of '92 and '93" about revolution and the dispossessed. "You million Christs with soft dark eyes," he wrote. He enjoyed the thought of writing it in Mazas Prison. That he was being observed did not trouble him a bit. He was always being observed by posterity.

Rimbaud had been something of a success up to then. He was the star pupil in his school. He won prizes for Latin verses. It protected him and his brother, both mere day pupils with the smell of the peasantry about them, from the consequences of their trouble making. The school favoured the wealthy paying borders but they won no prizes. Rimbaud, increasingly bohemian and defiant, was a hero to the other day boys because he beat the toffs. His role as prize winner also kept his pushy mother at bay. He hung around the cafes drinking and smoking, sometimes meeting up with a new teacher not much older than himself with a bohemian reputation and a love of poetry. George Izambard, like Rimbaud, was stifling in provincial France.

Rimbaud loathed Charleville. He hated its brightly-buttoned bourgeoisie flattening their bums on the benches in the square He loathed his mother and the dark Catholic home she had made with its heavy mahogany furniture fat with propriety. His father had run away from it years before. Mme Rimbaud had then put all her energies into shaping Arthur. His success at school increased her ambitions for him. She dressed him in prim, tight suits and smarmed his hair down when he went to accept his prizes. Even at fifteen she frequently boxed his ears. His only refuge had been the stinking privy at the end of the garden. Here he read *Les Miserables* until she found out. The book was banned in France. She summoned Georges Izambard for an explanation. She started to make plans to find Arthur a suitable occupation. But Rimbaud was finding refuge in ideas, in Hugo, Proudhon and Verlaine. The sunlit uplands of the Parnassians were in view. He would be a poet and a wanderer like his father. He discovered his father's old boots and overcoat in the damp farmhouse she had deserted in favour of an apartment in Charleville, to keep her children out of contact with the peasantry. She chose to ignore the overcoat he wore during the summer holiday but nagged him incessantly about employment. A nice job pushing a pen in the Town Hall would be ideal. She was a woman who never smiled and never had a kind word for anyone. Quoting Hugo, Rimbaud called her "the mouth of darkness." To the end of his life she remained immoveable, cold, undefeatable. He never escaped from her. Perhaps she deserved a son like Arthur Rimbaud.

Now, alone in his cell in Mazas Prison, Rimbaud revelled in the austere lines of its architecture. He soaked up the stark impact the featureless, battleship-grey stone walls had on him. They surpassed the most colossal conceptions of modern barbarity. He stood contemplating the graceless little deal table and solitary chair. It was a seer's cell! The lack of any pretension to humanity thrilled him. He lay in his hammock looking up at the unreachable window piercing the massive outer wall which leaked a flat light into the space. It was a view that invited strange perspectives and illusions. It was the prow of a ship sailing into non-entity. From the two ends of the room harmonic elevations connected. The scene facing him was a psychological succession of cross sections of friezes, atmospheric layers, and geological strata. Here he had escaped out of reach of the sour liquor that leaked from the furnishings of his mother's home and blackened his veins. Prison was freedom from that remorseless bourgeois striving. He suddenly had nothing left to fear.

While Arthur Rimbaud lay in the prison hammock, ten thousand young men and boys lay dead on the battlefield of Sedan, a few miles from Charleville. Thousands more were slowly dying from the septicaemia that infected their wounds. The Emperor, who had been captured after the defeat, was supping with Bismarck. The Second Empire had collapsed. Outside in the streets the *canaille* proclaimed the Republic which was swiftly taken under the control of the same bourgeois conservatives who had allowed the war to proceed unopposed. Arthur, grown bored, had written to Izambard who sent the Governor money to cover all expenses with verification that Rimbaud was not yet sixteen. He was put on a train to Douai, north of Paris, where the teacher's three spinster aunts lived. The following day the *canaille* arrived at the gates of Mazas Prison and forced the release of Émile Eudes and other political prisoners. Monelle, in a red dress and Mlle Michel with a sabre in her hand were at the head of the mob.

Arthur Rimbaud knocked on the pale-green door of a villa in Douai and was welcomed by an old lady. Before her stood a grubby urchin with a recently shaved head that made it easier to see the lice behind his ears. Izambard was not at home.

"I am the poet Arthur Rimbaud," said Arthur.

The woman took a deep breath and let him in. He brushed past her. She followed him down the hall noticing the smell

When Rimbaud saw the open door of the library he struggled out of his overcoat, dropped it in the doorway, walked in and began pulling books off the shelves and tossing them onto a desk. When he turned there were three almost identical old women looking at him. One of them held his overcoat at arm's length.

"I'll need a tobacco pipe and twenty grams of Caporal Dark Shag tobacco," he said, as if he needed the items to do some urgent work for them. And then,

"A first edition of *Les Fleurs du Mal* eh?"

He waved the book accusingly under their noses. His hands were filthy. He started riffling eagerly through the pages. The first edition contained six poems excised for obscenity in subsequent printings after an infamous trial during which the book had been defended by no less than Victor Hugo. He sat down with his elbows on the desk and buried his nose in it. After all inquiries had been met with grunts for some minutes the maid was sent out for the pipe, some tobacco and a large bar of powerful laundering soap. One of the aunts pulled a chair up beside him and, without a word, started picking the lice off his stubbly, filth encrusted head and crushing them between her thumbnails. After a while the grubby little boy smiled and shut his eyes. The thumbnails clicked away methodically.

When Izambard arrived the next day, the library windows were open and a smell of strong tobacco was on the air of the shrubbery. Arthur was looking spruced-up in some old clothes of Izambard's that he had grown out of as a teenager. The aunts seemed delighted with the boy. They had raised Izambard, There were three of them and the maid. They were just about up to coping with Arthur Rimbaud. He looked up at Izambard from his place at the desk as if he had never seen him before. He was in the depths of a literary quest through Hugo, Baudelaire, Racine, Shakespeare, Cervantes, Homer, Plutarch and Ovid. He was on the track of something. He had a copy of Verlaine's *Les Fêtes Galantes* in his hand. Izambard felt suddenly that he was now the outsider in the household. Rimbaud had the manner of one who had at last found a home.

Rimbaud soon got his feet under the desk from which Izambard edited a local newspaper too. Douai was in a war fever. News from Paris was frequent and confused. Izambard joined the National Guard. Rimbaud signed up as well, and deserted within a couple of weeks when his mother demanded his return to Charleville. Izambard decided to take him home personally after Arthur nearly lost him his job at the paper by writing a revolutionary account of a Douai Council meeting in Izambard's name. Meanwhile Rimbaud copied out the poems from his piss-stained notebook and gave them to a friend of Izambard's who was the part owner of a Paris publishing company. His mind was on poetry, not war. He had sent the Parnassian poet Théodore Banville some verses in the conventional style earlier in the summer. A feeble response from Banville led him to reject the Parnassians out of hand. Now he included a scatological verse about Venus in delicate Parnassian quatrains describing a balding goddess with an ulcer on her anus. With it he included a satire on the deposed emperor and a poem with a machine gun in it, perhaps the first mention of this weapon in literature. Rimbaud was preparing for war, but not with the Prussians.

After receiving the blistering reply to his letter informing Mme Rimbaud of Arthur's whereabouts, Izambard took Arthur back to Charleville. Georges was not invited into the house. Arthur, with his ears still stinging from the slaps around the head his mother gave him, sat down in his bedroom and started to write a poem about the joys of adolescence, "No one is serious when they're seventeen." He told her he would live in the derelict quarry on the edge of town if she threw him out for not getting a job.

The Rimbaud household settled into a bitter cessation of hostilities. When Arthur came in he went straight to his room after eating the cold dinner he found in the pantry. School did not reopen; the school-house was being used as a hospital for wounded soldiers. He mooched around the cafes. He wrote graffiti with charcoal on walls around town:

I have hung ropes from belfry to belfry; garlands from window to window; gold chains from star to star, and I dance,[2]

He reconvened "the brotherhood of bohemian filth," as he called it, with his friend Ernest. They ventured into the country. They walked along the lanes in the late September sunlight reading the poems of Victor Hugo aloud to each other. In Charleville the band was absent from Station Square, the top hats and balloon bums were nowhere to be seen. Arthur loved it. He preached apocalypse to his friend. They fell in with any wastrel, deserter or vagabond they met and shared their tobacco with him in exchange for the brusque wisdom of the dispossessed. Within a week Rimbaud went on the road.

He had less than a franc and just one bar of chocolate in his pocket, but he had the sense to put on a pair of winter long-Johns, one of his father's old waistcoats and to take his battered bowler hat with him. He had listened to the advice of a tramp on the virtue of being too warm over being too cold. He put a spare pair of socks in the pocket of his overcoat with a copy of the poems of Paul Verlaine borrowed from the library in Izambard's aunts' house. It was the first week in October, a golden Indian summer

Arthur Rimbaud had never slept out in the open before. He followed the Marne valley along the road towards the Belgian border. He dawdled. He sat by the river out of sight all the first afternoon in the late sun, watching the water flow and reading from *Les Fêtes Galantes.* He started a poem in a new note book. The day grew stiller and cooler and then dark. The stars beset him, he thought; a swarm of stars about his ears. He wept a little with the pleasant emotion of being quite alone and lost. He was a savage, a solitary wanderer on the face of the earth. He walked up and down for a while shouting every obscenity he knew into the silence. He stood on the bank and masturbated slowly, eventually ejaculating into the water. Then he curled up in his overcoat and slept like a baby until dawn.

In truth I have wept too much. The dawns were harrowing.[3]

In the early mist he drank river water and splashed his face.

The magic event plays at the top of an amphitheatre crowned with thickets.[4]

He lit his pipe and walked slowly back towards the road. He walked north through a landscape of vague forested hills. The river appeared and reappeared in unsuspected places, rolling through the silent valley. Slowly the sun warmed away the mist. Arthur Rimbaud saw no one for hours. He sat by the roadside with his boots and socks off cooling his feet, happily writing a poem in the notebook. The villages appeared to be deserted. Slowly a curious malaise grew in him, a shortness of breath and a slight dizziness, perhaps brought on by hunger. The landscape seemed to be flowing like the river. At a bend in the road a stand of pines above the bank writhed about in a momentary breeze.

"A sickening mystery of yesteryear," said Arthur Rimbaud.

His voice seemed entirely to fill the place. The slight sensation of a shortness of breath intensified until he identified it as fear. The valley seemed to be echoing with silence.

He thought of olden times, dungeons and knights at arms:

Oh what can ail thee knight-at-arms,

Alone and palely loitering?

Something was happening. He felt a shock. For a moment he rocked on his feet. He sat down in the road. He had the overwhelming sensation that the entire landscape was inside his own skull, that when he looked at it he was looking at himself. It was like staring into his own eyes in a mirror. A rush of adrenaline made him gasp. He tried to shake the world out of his head. A raucous cacophony beset his ears. It came into focus as the sound of hundreds of rooks cawing. He got up, cursing, and filled his pipe. Through the tracery of leaves he could see fields of blackcurrants along the river, the dying leaves a deep red. The rooks swarmed above the pines along the field margins. He thought:

"The dear delicious crows!"

Then the crows seemed to burst the confines of his skull and the world spilled out again. Rimbaud lit his pipe and started walking.

He found a bar open in a village. The only customer was an old peasant with a stump for a leg drinking in the corner. His crutches stood against the wall. Rimbaud spent his last few sous on two litres of cider in a curious gourd-shaped stoneware flagon. He tied it up in his scarf and slung it over his shoulder. He found a place out of sight from the road among hazel coppice in the warm, green afternoon mist and sat down to drink. The elms along the road were completely still. The light became dull. He drank the curious golden liquor until the pressure in his chest lifted. He drank it all. He started to sweat. He lit his pipe. It made him vomit into the heather. Presently he fell asleep.

Blackcurrant River

Unheeded, blackcurrant river rolls

Through strange valleys

To the sound of a hundred crows,

True good voices of angels,

And the great moving of the pines

When several winds plunge into them.

Everything rolls with these disgusting mysteries,

The fields of olden times,

The dungeon tours, the grand parks.

Along these banks you understand

The dead passions of knights-at-arms.

Ah! But the winds are curative!

The walker looks through the tracery

He'll proceed with more courage now.

Soldiers of the forest, the Lord's messengers,

Dear delightful crows

See off that cunning peasant

Drinking a toast to his old stump! [5]

When he awoke the stars were out. He felt the dew touch his face. He sat up invigorated. He still felt a little drunk. He set off into the night, seeming to hear the stars swish softly about the sky. At about nine o'clock he knocked on the door of a school friend who lived in a village not far from the Belgian border.

The boy's parents saw a grubby cherub in a scarecrow's coat. He looked as if he were playing the part of a tramp in a play. There was even hay on his collar. And he had rather disturbing grey-blue eyes with the whites distinctly bloodshot. Their own boy was sitting at his desk over some Latin homework. Rimbaud pushed himself into his school friend's chair and without a word started correcting the work.

"I'm hungry," he said. "Get me something to eat."

The next morning he set off with some money he had been given and directions to a cousin in an army post up at the border who would surely take him in for the night.

Rimbaud took two days to cover the short distance. It was warm enough at night. He wrote sonnets. He took long diversions through the forest.

In the woods there is a bird, his song makes you stop and blush [6]

He tried to recreate the sensations he had experienced the previous day. He followed geometric inclinations. The track was a tangent to the sky. Up there, following the little costumed troop, he discovered a hollow in the ground and a nest of small white animals; and later a silent grandfather clock in a glade of oaks.

He ate chocolate and slept on the leaves. Just before dawn the smell of earth wakened him like a shout. He rolled to his feet and started walking. The shadow camps on the woodland road had not yet been struck. He walked awakening warm and living breaths, and the precious stones looked and the wings lifted without a sound.

I am the one who walks the high road through the stunted woods; the noise of the sluice gates drowns out my footsteps. For a good while I can see the melancholy golden wash of dawn. [7]

His hunger, like scraps of black air ringing blue, pulled his stomach. He walked, singing nonsense:

"Anne, Anne, my hunger

Flee on your donkey."

He got lost. He seemed to have been walking all day. The pebbles washed across the track looked like small loaves of bread. He got down on his hands and knees and ate some earth. He shouted,

"Dinn! dinn! dinn! dinn! I eat air, rock, earth, iron. Turn my hungers!"

He wrote in his notebook.

"The paths are rough. The knolls are covered with broom. The air is still. How the birds and springs are far away! It can only be the end of the world if you go on."

Eventually the river was before him again. He knelt in the mud and drank for a long time. He walked on into a haze of hunger and exhaustion. The cabin where his friend's cousin lived was empty. He ate the loaf he found there and slept in the bunk. The next morning he crossed the border into Belgium.

At the first town there was a railway station on the line to Charleroi. He walked in and bought a ticket from a reluctant counter-clerk:

"My dear chap, I am a journalist returning from the Prussian front."

He entered a little carriage with pink decorations and blue upholstery. He sat in his muddy clothes and smiled unnervingly at a family with a teenage girl in a bonnet and silks. He imagined slipping his hands under her clothes. The family did their best to ignore him but he kept muttering. The girl was sneaking glances at him. She blushed. He had beautiful eyes and seemed to be fondling something in his pocket.

In Charleroi Rimbaud arrived at the home of another boarding student from his school whose father was a senator in the Belgian parliament and the publisher of a progressive newspaper. The maid took his wretched overcoat. He sat down and silently wolfed the dinner he was invited to eat with the family. They had a daughter. She watched the boy with the ice-blue eyes who stared belligerently back at her. His table manners were disgusting. His hands were filthy. He belched and wiped his streaming nose with his sleeve. He took possession of the wine and drank most of the bottle, gulping his glasses down in one swallow. Then he began talking. He called Thiers, the new leader of the French bourgeois republicans, a "prick." He replied to questions from the father of the household in a startlingly good imitation of his strong Belgian-French accent. He farted and said "The Bishop has spoken!" He offered his services as a revolutionary journalist. When he started on the brandy before he had been offered any the girl was sent to bed and he was asked to leave. Well-fed and staggering a little, Arthur found himself a bench in a nearby park and fell into a deep sleep.

He hung around Charleroi for a second night, drinking beers and eating sandwiches in a carter's tavern called The Green Inn. Here the barmaid gave him a kiss. He wrote a sonnet about it and read it to her.

"A full week I had been on the road, feet

Swollen and blistered. Made it to Charleroi

Stopped off at the Green Inn, ordered some

Ham rolls and a tall glass of draft beer."

Rimbaud walked to Brussels, a distance of forty miles, the next day. He had been unable to find a carter at the inn who would take him there for free. At nearly midnight, exhausted and filthier than ever he knocked on the door of a friend of Izambard's whose address he recalled from a conversation. He begged shelter in Izambard's name. He stayed two nights. The mother of the household fussed over him and persuaded him to bathe. The next morning she provided him with a new suit of clothes. They were the broad lapelled velvet jacket, waistcoat and silk tie we see him in in the photographs taken in Paris the following year. She found him a suitcase for his old clothes. She gave him enough money for the train to Douai. The following day Rimbaud walked the streets of Brussels looking almost normal, save for the prison hair-cut and the angry blue stare. On a green bench in the park a pale Irish girl sang and played the guitar. She sang in French under huge white cumulus clouds moving across an intensely blue sky. She sang *Les Temps des Cerises:*

"The gay nightingale and the mocking blackbird shall sing

And lovers have the sun in their hearts,"

Arthur Rimbaud took out his notebook. He wrote:

"A thousand blue devils dance in the air."

Chapter Three

The House of Lost Children

Monelle and L'Oursin got the circus animals out of Paris in mid-September before the Prussian army had fully encircled the city. The Master had family on a farm in the Ardennes in the Meuse valley not far from Charleville. The five ring ponies, the dogs and three cart horses were taken to the Canal Saint Martin and put on a big coal barge. A small caravan was also got aboard and the lot concealed under canvas sheeting. Paris was still being supplied from the north and the canal network was active. Once safely beyond Paris they became simply a travelling show. They performed in villages along the way where they pastured the animals in exchange for the entertainment. They performed in Station Square, Charleville, a couple of days before Rimbaud returned there from Douai. On their way back down the valley, carrying only blankets and a guitar and saxophone with them, they saw him enter a village bar. L'Oursin pointed out the ragged youth to Monelle. Rimbaud did not notice them where they stood quietly at the corner of the road; he was a tangent to all spheres.

They busked their way back towards Paris, sometimes sleeping out, more often guests in an inn or village barn. They took local advice about concentrations of troops. It was not difficult to move unobserved between the assembling battalions. They avoided main roads, crossing the stubble of harvested fields, most of the grain from which was to end in Prussian hands. They slowly negotiated a way to the West, increasingly avoiding habitation and sleeping among the vines or in the woods. Eventually Paris could be seen, its spires and chimneys vague in the soft September light. By this time they were half-starved and very wary, on the lookout for nervous defending forces in forward positions. There were none. They simply found a way through the bastions which were in a shocking state of disrepair and manned by a few National Guard who signalled directions to pass such defences as there were. Paris lay undefended two weeks after the defeat at Sedan, and was filling up with disaffected troops fleeing the Prussians. The same gouty martinets that had flattered the Emperor into war now established themselves in command of Paris. In the event they had nothing to fear. Bismarck had no intention of fighting his way through the streets. He planned to lay siege until the new bourgeois government capitulated. Negotiations were already underway.

On the heights of Montmartre the circus was battening down for the coming storm. The tent had been stored in sections in different locations around Montmartre. Equipment was dispersed. The caravans and trailers remained, but there was no work. The Master would feed them as long as he was able. But they chose to shift for themselves. After Monelle had seen the old perfumer they took their instruments and ran back down the hill to *La Marmite*.

La Marmite, "the Pot," was part of a network of mutual societies and cooperatives in working class northern Paris that included a bank. It was a cooperative kitchen and café. A strongly built woman stood at the door wearing a fisherman's sweater with the sleeves rolled up, a broad army-issue belt cinching in a short red skirt. There were clogs on her feet and a Prussian infantry beret pushed back over thick coifs of braided blond hair on her head. She was smoking a cigar.

"Monelle!"

She was delighted to see the girl, and the musical instruments.

"Come in and sing for us!"

"We didn't eat for a couple of days."

"Then eat!"

Inside, the ground floor comprised a café and a big kitchen. The building, in a shabby lane in Pigalle at the foot of Montmartre, was a warehouse, with small derricks on the two upper floors for lifting sacks into storage. The food cooperative bought in bulk and numbered farmers among its members. For a few sous a week members were guaranteed enough to eat. The café provided food at cost or free to all comers, destitute children among them.

The street kids were much in evidence. Attracted to the free food they had occupied a derelict building near *La Marmite.* The Cooperative helped them out with bedding and fixed the leaks. The squat became known as The House of Lost Children. There were thousands of lost and abandoned children in Paris as a result of the war. Mlle Michel found households around Montmartre for many who arrived there and they attended her school which had doubled in size catering for refugee children.

The more rebellious kids stayed on in The House of Lost Children. They hung around *La Marmite* and occupied themselves with petty crime and politics. The cooperative fed them and gave them love and moral council. One of their mentors was Monelle. The kids, between six and twelve years old, ran the House of Lost Children pretty well on their own. And they were never so happy as when they were the heart and soul of *la canaille,* the mob. They were at Mazas Prison when Eudes was freed. A few days later they were among the crowd that invaded the Legislative Council and forced the creation of a Republic amid talk of a watered-down constitutional monarchy. Power was briefly in their hands, but they cared even less for it than they did for money. Justice is the lust of the mob. But power they wielded. A couple of hundred people, quite a few of them children, created the Third Republic. They are invisible to history, many of those who make it from below.

La Marmite started to fill up on the news getting about that there would soon be music there. The Lost Children claimed corners and vantage points. The windows steamed up. The atmosphere was festive, but no one was drinking. Alcohol was not served there. Usually the café catered for the old and for mothers with young children. It was always warm and safe. Three local National Guard came in, wearing scruffy blue uniforms, smoking, and a little drunk, with some of the nearby shopkeepers including the shoe-maker and the printer. The girls from Place Pigalle turned up.

L'Oursin pushed back his plate and opened his saxophone case. He dropped a reed into his glass of water to wet it up. Monelle tuned her guitar and played Liebestraum by Liszt from memory. Mlle Michel had given her the music. The room went completely quiet. The National Guard listened with their mouths open. L'Oursin fixed the reed onto the mouthpiece and joined her. The strange golden instrument looked like a modern alchemical apparatus. But it sounded like a voice. The reed cut curves and volumes into the melody like the shape of the instrument itself. . It sounded like the cry of revolution to the dispossessed in the room. Monelle sang *Le Crie du Peuple,* and all the rebel songs. They played nonstop for nearly two hours. About half way through Louise Michel arrived with some of the older pupils from school. She pushed her way through the crowd and joined Natalie Lemel at the door to the kitchen. A shout of "Vive Louise!" went up from the majority of women and children in the room.

As always, Michel was astonished at L'Oursin's playing. He could play anything. He had learned to read music easily and had played much of the dissonant and strange music Michel herself composed, accompanied by her at the piano. They played Rameau together. They improvised freely whenever they got the chance. Now he was faultlessly harmonizing the songs Monelle sang, and between songs he improvised themes from the opera or the street; rhapsodies of obscure melodies, martial music, and vendor's cries. He launched into Arab music learned from an Algerian illusionist at the circus, while Monelle shook a tambourine and the kids danced.

When the music ended Michel got up to speak. She told them the latest news from Victor Hugo about the state of the defences and the corruption of the contractors appointed to repair them. She ridiculed the Government of National Defence. She cursed the sudden leap in prices that were driving the poor of Paris into hunger before the siege had really begun. She called for Montmartre to descend on the hoarders and profiteers in the bourgeois arrondissements. She cried revolution and invoked the Commune. She finished with this, looking directly at the National Guard who often spent their wages on drink while the women supported their families:

"The old world ought to fear the day when women finally decide they have had enough. They will not slack off. Strength finds a refuge in them. Beware of them! Beware of those who go across Europe waving the flag of liberty. Beware of the most peaceful daughter of Gaul now asleep in the deep resignation of the fields. Beware of the women when they are sickened by all that is around them and rise up against the old world. On that day the new world will begin!"

Another woman spoke up, denouncing the priests, and then another. The evening debate at *La Marmite had* got underway.

Monelle, Michel and her pupils were brought back in triumph to the House of Lost Children. Monelle agreed to stay the night. The kids had successfully begged the crowd at the café and counted out over a franc in sous on the floor by candle light. When Louise tried to steal a couple of coins there was uproar and demands for a story. She told them a story about druids and the wolves of Haute Marne. The children had been given small pallets made by a local mattress maker, clean and stuffed with a little lavender among the horse-hair, which were now pulled up in an arc around a wood-burning stove that had been placed in the centre of a big dry room on the second floor of the building. A stack of wood was piled beside it in anticipation of winter. There was a big draughty attic above, which Monelle had decreed should be left free for the bats which clustered on the rafters. It was used, nevertheless, by some of the older kids who wanted to get away on their own. All the children had been persuaded that bats were the guardians of street kids everywhere.

Many of the children were slowly emerging from deep trauma. Local women and the workers at *La Marmite* did their best to nurse them back to health. Some were slowly dying of tuberculosis. Consumption walked the streets of nineteenth century Paris like the angel of death. But the kids had found a place, perhaps only possible close to an experiment in self-help like the Cooperative, where a successful welfare system had been created, more or less out of nothing, by the poorest people in the city. One of the members of the collective was a doctor.

The older, more politically engaged kids put up wall posters for a little extra income, a plug of tobacco, or a bottle of wine. They worked for the political Clubs that were emerging across Bellville, Pigalle, Montmartre and Les Batignolles. They put up posters for the Vigilance Committees, the clubs and the International Working Men's Association. Wall posters remained the primary organizational medium for the dispossessed until well into the following century. They fly-posted news of the meetings of a new organization called The Central Committee of the Twenty Arrondissements, the name echoing the Central Committee of the French Revolution. It was an association of republican and revolutionary small businessmen, tradesmen and workers that was seeking a way to influence events. It called for a Republic that would refuse to negotiate with the Prussians while they were on French territory. The Government of National Defence, more frightened of its own revolutionary poor than the Prussians, sought an accommodation with Bismarck.

By the end of September the effects of the siege were being felt across the city. Telegraphic and postal communications had been cut. One day the printer near *La Marmite*, gave the kids in The House of Lost Children hundreds of posters announcing the flight of a balloon from Place Saint-Pierre, on the edge of the heights of Montmartre. Two balloons rose into the early morning air and drifted west over the Prussian lines which they showered with leaflets. A band of Montmartre musicians, including Monelle and L'Oursin, played a piece written by Louise Michel called "On wings of Revolution." Michel stood beside Victor Hugo to watch the balloons lift off. He was fierce with nationalist and republican rhetoric while the more skilled among the lost children made good use of the crowd of bourgeois enthusiasts assembled. Pocket-books and purses disappeared. One kid was collared and the local Federal Guard stepped in, arrested him and released him seconds later.

The successful breaking of the communications blockade initiated a pigeon post that used the new science of microfilm to reduce hundreds of letters to a manageable size. The people of Paris needed something to cheer them. The first sorties attempted by the generals appointed to defend Paris had been routed by the Prussians. The city was thick with rumour that the Government was about to capitulate. It was getting cold, and the poorest were beginning to starve.

Michel and one other teacher were now looking after two hundred children at the school on Rue Odot. Louise's mother looked after the little ones, some as young as three, with help from the older pupils. No one was turned away. Michel forced the Mayor of Montmartre, Georges Clemenceau, whom she and Hugo knew well, to provide for her children throughout the siege. Louise Michel was not a woman easily refused. And Clemenceau was a revolutionary of sorts. He ordered a separation of church and state in the schools under his jurisdiction. Rebellious Montmartre was in any case fiercely anti-clerical. From the beginning of the siege churches had been appropriated by the people to be used as political clubs that also provided a little warmth and food to the destitute families that crowded into them. The priests were driven out, and the nuns forced from church schools by gangs of women, some brandishing swords. The clubs were run from the bottom, unlike the more hierarchical Vigilance Committees or the International, which were organized by educated revolutionaries. Anyone could speak from the pulpit at the clubs, from the rag-picker to the small shopkeeper. There was no agenda and no formality, but decisions were taken, solidarity confirmed.

Louise Michel, Monelle and L'Oursin attended a club in *Saint-Pierre de Montmartre.* There were glasses and bottles on the altar, and half a kilo of free tobacco in the font. The Virgin had been dressed in the uniform of a combat nurse, with a pipe in her mouth. The talk was about local men, husbands and lovers who had been lost in the recent sorties. There was almost no medical attendance on the battlefields. How were ambulances to be found? There and then, from the pulpit, Michel organized her own sortie from Montmartre into the bourgeois district of west Paris in time for mass. She selected a particularly thuggish-looking Federal, borrowed a rifle from another, and with L'Oursin, Monelle and half a dozen kids from the House of Lost Children walked down to the Champs Élysées. They entered a church in the middle of mass. Michel, her head uncovered, rapped on the floor with her rifle butt and told the priest to "shut up." They took a considerable amount of money from the terrified congregation. They moved on to shake down a jewellers shop and other businesses. Montmartre had "descended on Paris" as the wealthy feared it would.

It was not long before some soldiers loyal to the bourgeois cause started to threaten the clubs. They arrived to disrupt a meeting Michel was chairing. They were all fully armed with sword-bayonets fixed. Michel reached into the drawer of the table she sat at, produced a revolver and pointed it at the leading soldier's head.

"If you are not cowards shoot me now," she said, "all I have ever deserved is a little slug of lead. Don't hesitate! I will count to ten and then fire."

She started counting. They left.

The lost children were well supplied with demonstrations to chase during the first month of the siege. Mlle Michel herself led one to the *Hôtel de Ville.* The women of Montmartre asked to speak with the Governor; they demanded arms. Michel was arrested. Victor Hugo, who was in the building, obtained her release. The demonstrators were shouting for Commune when she came out. She told Monelle, L'Oursin and the lost children what happened on the way back to Pigalle and Montmartre.

"A colonel, regular and stupid features, square shoulders, square body, a shining example of a colonel, came to interrogate me. Nothing doing. A fat little jackass came in later, egged on by his own curiosity. I told him the poor of

Paris were weeping blood. The babies had no milk while the Governor kissed the Bishop's flesh and stuffed himself with mutton." [8]

In October it started to get cold. From the door of L'Oursin's little cabin on the heights of Montmartre it was possible to see Paris below, the opalescent mists at street level and the lilac smoke going straight up from the chimneys of those who had fuel; the coal-fire red sunrises lighting up the frost. He spent some hours each day repairing a small collection of saxophones he had acquired through crooked dealings with the military bands. L'Oursin had learned some metal working after visiting the workshop of the crusty and embittered inventor of the instrument. M. Sax, who was at the time nearly bankrupt with the expense of defending his patents from other instrument makers, tolerated L'Oursin, who played better than he did and who impressed him by demonstrating an extension of the upper range of the instrument into the altissimo register. He paid L'Oursin to test his design modifications with the gift of a few tools, know-how and solder.

Usually, when the days warmed up, L'Oursin put panniers on the mule, the circus's only remaining animal, and went looking for wood. In the Bois de Boulogne the trees were coming down. The authorities tried to protect the Emperor's newly landscaped civic space from the population with little success. People were prepared to fight for fuel. The mule was a valuable ally. It bit and kicked anyone who approached, and if L'Oursin had to run, it would find its way back to Montmartre alone. He supplied The House of Lost Children the perfumer and the circus with wood.

He also organized the lost children and made sorties with some of them into the no-man's-land between the ramparts and the Prussian line, which was dug in beyond cannon range. They went at night to search for the food or coal to be found in abandoned farms. They found the occasional pig, which they slaughtered and cut up on the spot.

One morning the mule returned alone to the circus with an injured child in one of its panniers. The doctor for the Cooperative removed a bullet from the boy's leg. Six children and L'Oursin were missing. This was at the time that Gustave Flourens, a revolutionary adventurer who had taken part in the Cretan Insurrection a couple of years earlier, descended on the *Hôtel de Ville* with five thousand of the Belleville National Guard whom he commanded. He demanded arms for the population and the creation of a Commune. The blimps did not appear to understand what he was saying, although five thousand men in arms at the door aroused their interest. Flourens, who commanded the Bellville guard, proffered his resignation when his proposals were rejected. The National Guard returned to the Belleville ramparts. The children missed the fun, holed up in The House of Lost Children, miserable and grieving.

Then L'Oursin and three other children turned up. They were exhausted and their teeth were chattering. They had been captured by the Prussians, who determined to shoot the lot of them for spies. They were locked in a barn for two days while a decision was sought as to what was to be done with them. Eventually a Prussian soldier came in, tossed them half a loaf of bread and pointedly left the door open. They escaped that night. They desperately tried to locate the mule, which aroused the Prussians who began firing on them. L'Oursin and the four children closest to him fled. L'Oursin had to carry the injured boy. They soon discovered they had fled further behind the Prussian line. They came back through the following night and in the morning, safely beyond range, the mule found them. Two children never returned.

That night, despite his exhaustion, L'Oursin performed with Monelle at *La Marmite* where he demonstrated a bass saxophone loaned to him by the inventor. The crowd called it *La Belle Joséphine* after the great gun, the largest in Paris, on Mont-Valérien. M. Adolphe Sax, a Belgian, who had been given a harsh time by French instrument makers, including an attempt on his life, since he had won the competition for new military instruments, was delighted when L'Oursin told him. He was not so happy to learn the instrument was out of tune in the lower register.

"Lengthen the bell," said L'Oursin.

And he did, after throwing the annoying youth out of his workshop.

When the weather became even colder Monelle started sleeping in The House of Lost Children. She nursed a little girl dying of consumption, sleeping in her bed with her. Eventually she woke to find the child quite stiff and dead. The kids carried the coffin up to Montmartre cemetery themselves, but the ground was too hard to dig the grave. No one had told them. They brought the coffin back and put it up in the loft to be watched over by the bats, or so Louise Michel told them. The doctor was shocked, but there was nowhere else to put it. The body was quite frozen.

The temperatures dropped. Monelle and the children spent the long freezing evenings in the relative warmth of the clubs. They did the rounds, bringing with them food from *Le Marmite,* in particular salt herrings, which were to become an important food throughout the siege. One of the members of the Collective was a fisherman out of Le Havre. That summer he had brought a fishing boat filled with fresh herring up river to the city. The price offered in Le Havre was so low at the time that the captain donated his catch to the Cooperative. They salted the fish down in barrels in the warehouse, stinking up the entire neighbourhood with guts and causing packs of stray dogs to arrive. They salted the best part of a ton of fish, which was to keep many of the poorest in the 18th Arrondissement alive through the winter of the siege. Louise Michel was to recall at the end of her life that anyone could eat at the meeting halls but that two people might have to share one herring between them.

Towards the end of October the Seine froze. The lost children and Monelle flew around the icy black streets and lanes like bats, visiting clubs, cheering the rhetoric of the speakers. There was no work. Rents could not be paid. The poorest, prostitutes and rag-pickers driven together by the cold into places of debate with seamstresses and tradesmen started ordering their own lives. A free school was set up in the church of Saint-Pierre de Montmartre. A collective was formed to make uniforms for the National Guard. From the pulpits of "the black crows' barn" ragged women with mob caps on their heads and swords on their hips denounced the clergy and the bourgeoisie as one tyranny. Louise Michel, Nathalie Lemel and other educated revolutionaries spoke, but as equals among the illiterate and furious mob:

One of the older girls from The House of Lost Children who had escaped to the streets from a Church orphanage got up and cried:

"We must shoot the priests! To be married is to be a slave. Women who go to confession are lost. Grab the priests and burn their ugly mugs off! The same for the nuns!" [9]

Nathalie Lemel took her place in the pulpit. She spoke quietly and at length about forming cooperatives and of mutual aid. She ended:

"Frail women, you will nourish yourselves, clothe yourselves, you will become the powerful generators if a strong race." [10]

Across much of Paris the old order prevailed. But in the more militant quarters of the northern ghettoes a new world was being imagined. Pawn-shops were plundered and their goods returned to their owners. The concierges were driven out from a number of tenements and those that remained stopped asking for the rent.

Louise Michel presided over the Montmartre Vigilance Committee. It was an assembly charged with defending the interests of the community and protecting the gains of the emerging revolution. It was always packed with people. She quoted Hugo:

"Lazarus, Lazarus, Lazarus,

Rise up!"

She roused furious anguish with her rhetoric:

"It is the morning come of the new legend. Do you hear the wind that passes in the air? All of you that wear the iron collar; let's talk while we wait for the hour to strike! This earth is the charnel house of the peoples' dreams. This sombre life cradling sad days! I don't know when the final struggle between the old world and the new will take place. I only know I'll be there. And other revolutionaries will be there too. The spark will unite the whole world. Everywhere the crowds will rise up. Meanwhile we wait, and while we wait speeches will continue. These speeches are the rumbling of a volcano and when we least expect it the lava will erupt!"

At the end of these meetings the participants would often pitch out onto the freezing streets crying revolution. Spontaneous demonstrations broke out as people opened their doors and joined the crowd. Sometimes, amid the uproar, the National Guard would beat the two great drums of Montmartre which could be heard as far away as Notre Dame on a frosty midnight.

At the end October the Aurora Borealis was visible from Paris. It was red. It was taken to be a bad omen. The newspapers called it "the sky of blood." A couple of days later the city of Metz capitulated to the Prussians, and with it all hope that Paris might be rescued. The capitulation occurred after secret negotiations with the besieging Prussians. It fuelled suspicions that the Government of National Defence in Bordeaux was seeking an armistice with Bismarck, who now walked the gilded halls of the palace of Versailles, where the bourgeoisie who had fled Paris seemed to like him well enough.

One icy morning late in October the lost children, who had been running from club to club in increasing joy and anticipation, charged into *Le Marmite*. They had sticks, clubs and bayonets in their hands. The Cooperative was already on the move. The *canaille* had awoken. All over northern Paris crowds formed. Armed National Guard joined them, and a mass of people poured down into central Paris to the *Hotel de Ville*.

Monelle and L'Oursin took the guitar and the saxophone with them. The Montmartre *canaille,* led by a gang of unemployed building workers with iron bars in their fists, faced down a challenge from some troops loyal to the Government on the edge of *Place de Hôtel de Ville*. Behind them a party of National Guard carrying rifles with fixed bayonets confirmed the matter. By midday there were fifteen thousand people in the square roaring for Commune while the Government inside hastily cobbled some proposals for elections together. Some of the mob started banging on the doors. L'Oursin gave Monelle his saxophone and quickly gathered a few of the builders together. They levered a door off its hinges with the iron bars and the riffraff poured in.

They burst into the debating chamber in such numbers that it was impossible to move. A Blanquist Federal officer announced the Commune. The Government were arrested and put in an upstairs room from which the Governor was able to flee in the chaos. Flourens arrived and initiated a furiously divisive debate about whom to nominate for a Commune government. Victor Hugo was prominent among the names put forward. Old M. Blanqui himself arrived and was roughed up by the mob who thought he was a government minister and pulled his beard. All over the building, into the night, furious debates arose. The windows at the front were smashed open and the mob started hurling the furniture out of them. Mlle Michel, dressed as a man among the lost children, joined in, helping to tip an elaborate Imperial cabinet filled with government edicts onto the terrace below. Monelle and L'Oursin sat with many others on the window sills with their legs hanging out of the building and improvised a rhapsody that climaxed with the crowds singing the Marseillaise.

The night wore on. Slowly the mob thinned. It seemed all over. Flourens and a company of Belleville National Guard held the building. Towards dawn they were forced to retreat. The Governor was in the square with a regiment of Breton Mobiles, who were conservative peasants with no loyalty to the Paris working class.

For nearly twenty four hours complete anarchy and lawlessness held sway and no one had been injured.

Chapter Four

Class War

The invasion of the debating chamber in the *Hôtel de Ville* by the stinking *Canaille,* enabled by L'Oursin's quick thinking, may have changed the course of the Franco Prussian War. We are accustomed to believing that famous individuals dictate the course of history. But perhaps unknown individuals are the real authors of events. If L'Oursin had not forced the doors perhaps someone else in the mob would have done. But if Napoleon had not seized power in France, someone else would probably have done that too. The conditions for tyranny or the breaking down of a door remain the same. But it is Power that writes history and Power selects its own heroes.

In any event, the conviction in government that the Prussians were not the greatest enemy of bourgeois France grew from that moment and with it a resistance to any thought of arming the people of Paris. The city had the wherewithal to manufacture sufficient weapons. Any Paris mechanic had the makings of a gunner as the Commune was soon to show. There were men enough to double the size of the armies loyal to Church and property that the generals commanded. But the brass and the frock-coated *haut bourgeoisie,* who had deftly seized power after Sedan, when the *canaille* forced the creation of a new Republic, had more in common with their own class in Prussia than with the revolutionary classes in Paris. And there is a general truth here, one that the kids in the House of Lost Children understood fully. Capitalist armies are not primarily raised to fight other nations. They are there to control the very populations from which they are drawn. When the people rise up, the bourgeois combatants defining the spheres of influence of competing states will always join forces to crush freedom and change.

Bismarck, in negotiation for an armistice with the Government of National Defence in Bordeaux, would make no move towards peace while revolution arose unchecked in France. He had his own dispossessed to fear. Revolution would not so much weaken France as strengthen revolutionary Germany. In Paris, workers, tradesmen and intellectuals formed the Vigilance Committees and the over-arching Central Committee to protect the nation from its own bourgeoisie, to defend the infant Republic and to promote revolution.

Mlle Michel made arrangements to bury the dead girl as soon as the thaw came. There were more fresh graves in the cemetery, most of them without religious symbols to them. The lost children brought a red flag and planted it firmly on the mound of soil. But there were no flowers to be found in November.

"There are flowers in the churches," said Louise Michel, looking at the lost children.

They organized themselves into raiding parties. They went that night. In the morning the new graves in Montmartre cemetery were covered with the flowers that had been given to the churches from the greenhouses of the wealthy and the Botanical Gardens at the Tuileries Palace. But one raiding party returned badly beaten. A twelve year old boy had a broken arm, and a nine year old girl had her front teeth knocked out. They had gone as far as Notre Dame and been trapped in the cathedral by half a dozen church officials.

The *canaille* rose up in the House of Lost Children. They determined to descend on Notre Dame in a mob. Monelle and Mlle Michel failed to dissuade them, so Monelle and L'Oursin recruited half a dozen men from the clubs. They left Montmartre in the small hours, Monelle and L'Oursin wearing the costumes of Columbine and Harlequin.

There was no arguing with Monelle when she conceived of theatrical means of pillage and offense in the heart of Paris. She stole Louise Michel's revolver from her room in the school. L'Oursin replaced Harlequin's wooden sword with a sword-bayonet. The costumes were fantastical and elaborate, in the tradition of the Comedia dell'arte. They ran the couple of miles from Montmartre to the river in bare feet, silently, through the quietest and meanest lanes and alleys, and finally burst into the silent, dimly lit building.

Long shadows flew along the walls at the end of the nave as the churchmen roused up. L'Oursin and the men from the clubs ran the length of the great building as if entering the underworld and fought the priests with their fists while the kids methodically and grimly desecrated the side alters. They hurled the great bible from the pulpit and set fire to it by pouring wax on it from the fallen and guttering candles. Monelle, in the smoke flames and din, looked like a fantastically coloured angel descended into hell. She walked slowly up to the high altar and threw the tall candelabra and the cross to the ground. She placed the muzzle of the revolver against the groin of the crucified Christ and blew a ragged powder-blackened hole in it.

The explosion of a revolver discharged in that echoing space sounded like the end of the world. The priests fled. Monelle called everyone together and they ran, but not before L'Oursin stabbed his sword in the leg of an armed priest who made to fire on them from the door. The next day the papers were filled with accounts of an act of desecration performed by Algerian Zouaves who had deserted from the Imperial army after Metz had fallen. The London Times described their outlandish uniforms in detail.

The desecration of Notre Dame inflamed the xenophobia that possessed the wealthier quarters of Paris during the siege. Anyone with the slightest accent was considered to be a Prussian spy or a Muslim terrorist. The police in those areas started arresting anyone denounced as having a foreign accent. Sewer-men emerging from underground were arrested for speaking in Piedmontese dialect.

During the Indian summer in October, the Fashionable had enjoyed taking their carriages along the road around the ramparts to gaze at the distant Prussian lines through opera glasses. When Bismarck's artillery found the range of the redoubts, in the hope of hastening the capitulation of the city, they kept away. In any case, within a month the Parisian *demi-monde* who had not fled to Versailles were beginning to think of eating their horses. Meat had begun to run out as early as the beginning of October in spite of the thousands of head of cattle and sheep that had been driven into the Bois de Boulogne only a few weeks previously before the Prussians encircled the city. Perhaps much of that had been salted down and hoarded, but that did not prevent the commencement of an open season on almost any animal with red blood in its veins. The official ration of meat had been cut drastically. Horses were selected for military use and the rest were slaughtered. Pet animals followed. Butchers started to specialize in dog and cat meat. Further down the social scale rats were on offer.

The poorest were a little more humane. In any case they were accustomed to surviving on oatmeal or a herring and a slice of dark bread. Red meat had always been a rarity for them. In the House of Lost Children there was outrage at the slaughter of cats and dogs by the inhabitants of the new boulevards. They were capable of slaughtering a pig but not a pet. Their opportunistic raids along the Boulevards began to include the rescue of dogs and cats which ended up hanging around the House of Lost Children and *Le Marmite.* Somehow the former pets of the rich found a place in the hierarchy of need for scraps, a little below the position of the hens of the neighbourhood. The mule was rather more of an urgent consideration. An edict had gone out ordering the slaughter or requisition of mules and donkeys. L'Oursin brought him down from the circus field on the heights and he was stabled in the ground floor of the House of Lost Children. They continued making regular sorties with him into the no-man's-land north of the city.

The poor and insurrectional quarters of Paris were cut off from the conduct of the war. The troops in the city were drawn from the conservative provinces. Belleville and Montmartre descended on central Paris in a series of demonstrations demanding more vigorous sorties and a push to break the Prussian grip on the city. The Central Committee, the clubs and the vigilance committees opened subscriptions to buy guns. The cannon on the heights of Montmartre were increased in number and manned by the local National Guard under their own control even though General Clement-Thomas, "the butcher of '48," who had savagely suppressed the revolution then, had been appointed commander of all the Paris National Guard. His authority was acknowledged in the districts where the National Guard was called the "Bourgeois Guard" by the mob. Here he paraded along the Champs Élysées surrounded by the young dandies of the boulevards. In Montmartre and Belleville the National Guard had no such martial pride. They were dishevelled and mutinous, often wore no uniform at all and discussed orders before doing anything. They set the guns up facing the city.

The printer who gave the lost children work putting up revolutionary posters was a founder member of the Central Committee of the Twenty Arrondissements. It formed in September, and resolved that the Republic would not negotiate with Bismarck. It called for the arming of the population and for a Commune. The backbone of the Central Committee was his class of self-educated workers, small traders, craftsmen and artisans. He was a quick, nervous little man dearly loved by the lost children. He spoke to them as adults, allowed them to hang around and watch his press rolling and had trained one youth, now working, in setting type. He talked socialism. He explained the ideas of Marx, and had printed the first French translation of Capital a couple of years earlier. He was a member of the *Le Marmite* cooperative and a friend of Nathalie Lemel, who was a bookbinder and trades unionist who had led a number of successful strikes, one of which had delayed the publication of Marx's book. He explained the ideas of Proudhon and of Louis-Auguste Blanqui to them He was at heart a mutualist and a libertarian like Lemel. He lectured on Darwin, after passing around a glass jar filled with bonbons to smooth his way. He would stop the press in order to clarify a point. Both Monelle and L'Oursin had been educated by him. Most of the lost children who decided not to take up Louise Michel's offer of schooling were unable to read, but they understood a broad range of contemporary ideas after hanging around the press for a while.

The Central Committee met in the revolutionary clubs in Montmartre. These men, and a few women, including Lemel, were distinguished by their complete lack of class pretension. Cobblers, stone-masons and engineers rubbed shoulders with small businessmen, shopkeepers and revolutionary intellectuals, like Eudes and Blanqui. Many were poor, even ragged. It made no difference to their status. They were drawn from a large pool of active dissidents known for their ability, courage and principle. They bore the marks of collective struggle, a certain engrained taciturnity; an ability to listen, a confidence in their own ability. They infused what might have become very ideologically divided meetings with a sense of purpose. Many had highly developed political skills got through organizing labour action under dangerous conditions. They knew they needed to foster unity by seeking the broadest possible consensus. Their first proclamation back in September had been a masterpiece of brevity. And they were dangerous. By beginning to organize the local National Guard units across working class quarters of Paris they were creating a revolutionary militia. But no one held executive power. Their instincts were horizontal, not hierarchical.

M. Verdier, the printer, taught politics as class war. He told the lost children, while his press clattered out proclamations from the Central Committee calling for all-out war against the occupying forces, that the Prussian soldiers were workers like they were; that the workers of France and Germany should unite. He explained to them that the class interests of the German and French bourgeoisie were the same, just as the class interests of German and French workers were the same. He predicted that the two nation states would combine against their own dispossessed if the poor rose up and presented a real threat. He told them that the Emperor was drinking *eau de vie* with Bismarck while mothers on both sides mourned the loss of their sons. He argued that the military brass and the politicians of the

Government of National defence would not remain loyal to the republican cause if their wealth were threatened; they would make common cause with the priests, the country squires and a conservative peasantry to bring Louis Bonaparte back from exile.

The kids, of course, understood all this very clearly in their own way. The Prussian soldier who had left the door to the barn open was no surprise to them. His lined, prematurely-aged face was the face of one of their own people. When they made sorties along the boulevards of the new quarters they knew who their enemy was. Some of the girls had their own reasons for hating the gentlemen in frock coats and top hats who stared after them. The parades of immaculate, red-trousered troops led by plumed and braided popinjays on horseback did not look like soldiers to them. Running among the bustles and broadcloth promenading the Champs Élysées they were more inclined to shy a half-brick at the army than to cheer it. To them, real soldiers were the shabby, half-drunk National Guard of the neighbourhood whom they knew and trusted.

The wealthy knew well enough who their enemies were, although they sometimes romanticized them. The painting by Delacroix of Liberty Leading the People, which celebrated the revolution of 1830, depicted *Marianne,* the emblem of revolutionary France, bare-breasted and bare-footed with just such a *gamine* as one of the lost children at her side. There are times when art and reality merge. The painting was suppressed, but etchings of it circulated.

M.Verdier had one on the wall of his workshop. He pointed to the urchin brandishing pistols beside *Marianne.*

"There you are," he said, "and that is Mme Lemel!"

The kids started calling their forays onto the new boulevards "class war." They bowled loose cobbles under the feet of carriage horses, and threw filth at the dresses of the ladies. The older boys were quite capable of fighting their way out of trouble. When the sound of distant cannon-fire made the promenaders flinch they yelled warnings and laughed at the beautifully-dressed grovelling on the muddy pavements. They stole, anything, and for the joy of it. They were part of a supposed decay in the social fabric that filled the boulevards with hawkers and crippled soldiers. The wealthy started to stay at home. It was also still possible for the well-heeled to get out of Paris to Versailles. The new houses of Haussmann were being slowly boarded up.

The temperatures dropped again. It snowed. The lost children started going out bare-footed to save the shoes that had been found for them by *Le Marmite* and the clubs. In those days a pair of boots cost about a month's wages to the poor. They would fly into the café kitchen and crouch beside the cooking stoves, shivering, until rousted out to wash a few dishes or carry plates of food. But their main occupation of posting up notices for meetings and demonstrations soon became searching for fuel. When a baby froze to death in the arms of its mother while she queued for bread, *Le Marmite* and the clubs organized a network of fuel scavengers.

It was no longer safe to go out with the mule. They went out in pairs and carried as much they were able. In the night the men would fell one of the trees planted along the boulevards. The kids and the desperate poor followed and dismembered them like locusts. Each tree became the centre of a potential riot, and the police could do little to stop it. Green timber was stored to dry a little in the House of Lost Children before being rationed out. The kids climbed walls and raided the gardens of boarded-up houses, pulling down pergolas and fencing. They made a successful raid on a coal depot that was fast emptying into the cellars of the rich by bribing the night watchman with a cheap bottle of brandy; one thing never in short supply during the siege was alcohol. The National Guard from the immediate neighbourhood of *Le Marmite* rode shotgun on the more risky undertakings. The appearance of a couple of shabby, slightly drunk, down at heel citizens' guard, carrying old chassepot rifles with meter long sword bayonets fixed, went a long way to calm the ire of gentlemen in top hats witnessing a gang of grubby urchins tearing up the fencing in the park. When one of the lost children was captured and locked in the *Mairie* of a bourgeois quarter, a small detachment of Montmartre National Guard set out, fully armed, to bring him back. Mlle Michel was alerted and ran down to the Montmartre *Mairie* to inform Georges Clemenceau who managed to defuse a dangerous situation. The boy was set free.

The kids also made regular visits to the market at *Les Halles*. The great wrought-iron galleries, then less than ten years old, were almost empty. The servants of the rich negotiated tense deals with traders, and paid large sums for any fresh food on sale, for food there always was, kept out of sight. It was dangerous territory for the lost children, who ran the gauntlet of shouts and blows. But there was usually something to grab, or they filled sacks with rotten vegetables to feed the mule, or bones destined for glue factories to feed the dogs. Even taking this half putrid rubbish was considered to be theft. The dealers and porters were dangerous people to cross, but they were mostly drunk and slow on their feet. And there was more to be found there than garbage. One of the girls specialised in finding money. A big food market in a time of shortage attracts a lot of stuffed purses. She worked with another girl who kept watch while she got down and sifted through the straw and debris on the market floor by hand. She rarely came away without finding a few coins. These she gave to Nathalie Lemel. Money was quite useless to street urchins, who would only be accused of theft if they tried to use it.

Monelle and L'Oursin also lived largely without money. They felt less inclined to busk the wealthier districts as the class war intensified, and decided to entertain for free in Montmartre and Belleville. The turning point came after the insurgency that captured the *Hôtel de Ville,* when the bourgeois press responded to the call for arms from the impoverished quarters by mocking the National Guard for the evidence of rickets and tuberculosis in their ranks. The supposed commander of all the National Guard, General Clement-Thomas, was the source of this mockery. The frock coats and braid in the *Hôtel de Ville,* who had seized power from a divided Left when the mob had forced the proclamation of a Republic after the capture of the Emperor at Sedan, had a visceral loathing of the poor. What made it worse was that the accusations were evidently true. The poor in the northern ghettoes felt the insult more than the privations of the siege, and, through the political clubs, they were beginning to understand who the authors of their poverty really were. They had known it in their bones for generations, of course, but now they were learning that there was a modern, enlightened explanation for class; that it was not disposed by God to be accepted and suffered in humility, but that it was the result of a war being waged against them by the thieves of their labour.

Up in the circus field on the Heights the circus master was keeping his seamstresses in employment by spending his savings on new costumes. He lent them to L'Oursin and Monelle, and often came himself to play the vulgar, slapstick scenes from the *Comedia dell'arte* in the street. Or they would do the rounds of the clubs at night, disrupting debates with a routine that continued out into the street and attracted a mob of kids at their heels.

The Moulin de la Galette had closed early in September along with all the other commercial entertainment in Paris. Theatres, concert halls and café entertainments had been ordered to shut down. The edict was intended to show a proper denial of pleasure on the part of the leisured classes in response to the privations of the siege. The Master cared nothing for any of that. He did not see art as a service to its audience so much as a display of superiority to them and a rod to beat them with. The masked and fantastic characters he commanded had their origins in the middle ages and earlier. In his hands they became a company of Lords of Misrule, and the stock subjects of lust, old age and pomposity were politicised and made relevant. The material was improvised too. Both L'Oursin and Monelle introduced whatever themes they liked. They were as likely to lampoon the pomposity of the revolutionaries as that of the Government. Gustave Flourens and Louis-Auguste Blanqui, who both advocated a revolutionary elite, were frequent butts. They were mocked for proving to everyone that the individual genius and heroism that they espoused self-evidently fails. It was difficult to claim that a revolutionary vanguard was at all effective after the last two disasters at the *Hôtel de Ville*. Neither, to her delight, was Louise Michel spared. The Master had something to say, and she listened, and then took a more intense pleasure in following her own path. The Montmartre kids followed the comedy trio, and in particular Harlequin (who is, after all, none other than the Pied Piper) playing a saxophone through the miserable slushy streets. They warmed their imaginations on the colours and the language. The Master's little troop was a kernel of fire burning in the cold ashes of Montmartre. It was as if they had descended, demonic and angelic beings united, from a tumultuous heaven already stormed and taken by the *canaille*.

At the end of November scavenging for wood became a lot easier. In the Bois de Boulogne an army began to assemble which felled its own trees to build shelters and fires. The landscape looked war-torn. A pall of smoke hung over everything and reached to the heights of Montmartre.

Paris drowned in fog. L'Oursin and the toughest of the lost children took advantage of the reduced visibility and the chaos to raid the encampments for bits of firewood already cut up. Newly forged cannon were being dragged towards the ramparts. Government posters went up on walls across Paris proclaiming a sortie that would unite the capital with the armies in the provinces.

There were no dependable armies in the provinces, and the generals in the *Hôtel de Ville* knew it well enough, but they were certain it would all be over before Christmas. Negotiations with Bismarck were well underway and a mixture of pride folly and arrogance impelled them to do something. It was a matter of honour. The sortie would silence their critics, show Bismarck the power of French arms once and for all, and force his hand to come to a quick agreement. And war has its own momentum. The men and materials were there. The troops had all been equipped with new uniforms (the largest industry in Paris was clothing), and they looked splendid parading on the Champs Elysées, from their white puttees, red trousers and dark-blue jackets to the kepis on their heads and the polished steel of the long sword-bayonets on their rifles.

General Trochu, the governor of Paris, and General Ducrot, the head of the army, both had records of failure and incompetence culminating in the surrender after the battle of Sedan. The troops they commanded were disaffected and had lost to the Prussians already, sometimes more than once. The Prussians had dug in and were concentrated around Paris. They were battle hardened and victorious. Nevertheless, the French generals were sure that the sortie could not fail. Much of Paris was certain of it too. The wall posters had a slightly hysterical tone. Ducrot pledged to die before he ordered a retreat. There was even optimism in Belleville and Montmartre. For the first time units of the National Guard had been incorporated into the army. They were both revolutionary and nationalistic and keen to prove their worth. In the Bois de Boulogne L'Oursin and the lost children came upon their friends from Pigalle kitted out in new uniforms who began to help them collect wood.

A hundred and fifty thousand men, supported by four hundred heavy guns were to cross the Marne to the south east of Paris, break through the Prussian blockade and link up with the Army of the Loire, which at the time was considerably disorganized. To this end the army had to be made as mobile as possible. Troops were to carry their own provisions and were ordered to lighten their loads by leaving their blankets behind. It had been raining for days across the watershed of the Marne and Seine and the Marne was beginning to flood. Ducrot's engineer was unprepared. There was a delay while more pontoons were got from Paris. There was chaos as the army shivered in makeshift bivouacs without food. Officers lost contact with their men. Eventually the river was crossed after a delay of twenty four hours that alerted the Prussians across their positions. Nevertheless the Prussian-held village of Champigny was taken in an assault that included the Belleville and Montmartre National Guard, who were less dependent on orders from above than their comrades in the regular army. But Ducrot then hesitated for a day. The Prussians emptied Versailles of troops and retook their former positions with heavy losses among the National Guard. Ducrot ordered a retreat. Of the fifty thousand men engaged in the battle eight thousand were dead, among them two of the three *Le Marmite* National Guard. Gustave Flourens, who despite an arrest warrant out for him after the invasion of the *Hôtel de Ville* was fighting with the Belleville Sharpshooters, was arrested on the battlefield when he was recognized during the retreat.

While the army of Ducrot was struggling to cross the Marne, Louise Michel was with another deputation of women to the *Hôtel de Ville.* These were obscure, working class women from one of the clubs who had proposals for the defence of Paris to put to the Government of National Defence. They had approached the Women's' Vigilance Committee of Montmartre claiming a recommendation from a friend of Michel's. Michel later discovered they had no such recommendation, but she would have gone with them anyway, even with the certain knowledge that she would be arrested again. The officials at the *Hôtel de Ville* were incredulous that these harpies of the *canaille,* the pox-ridden scum of the northern slums, should have anything to say at all. But they recognized Michel, and assumed the deputation had been organized by her as she expected they would. She told them she had come with the women only out of solidarity with them, that she would not petition a government she no longer recognized and that the next time they saw her she would have an armed uprising behind her. She was arrested, of course, and the women forced from the building. But when a deputation of citizens, including the deputy chief of police for the northern arrondissements, the Blanquist Théophile Ferré, came for her she was promptly released again. The Government feared that Montmartre and Belleville would descend on Paris. It would have been the perfect moment for an uprising, with a defeated army led by discredited generals limping back into the city. But history is made by individuals, albeit often unknown and unaware of their roles, and no one was there to spark it off.

The House of Lost Children and *Le Marmite* were filled with potential sparks. The city was like a cocked pistol. Perhaps they were the flint in the jaws of a hammer that the deaths of the two local National Guard had pulled back another notch. The men had been drinking companions of L'Oursin and the first adults he was on equal terms with. They were guardians of the lost children and were part of a network of local National Guard who protected the clubs. L'Oursin and the church-raiders brought armfuls of flowers to the men's families who had no graves to lay them on. The circus master encouraged them to place two red flags at the corner of his field on the Heights and the flowers were laid there. The old perfumer poured a whole vial of concentrated essence at the spot. It was said that the fragrance lingered for years, and the place became known as the Federal's corner long after the circus had moved on. Monelle organized a ceremony to which the men's families came. Louise Michel read poems by Victor Hugo in the freezing rain. The gunners on the buttes fired a salute that terrified half of Paris after she arrived at the cannon and ordered them to do it. She then went to the *Mairie* and told Georges Clemenceau to tell his friends in the *Hotel de Ville* that the gunfire was the *canaille* of Montmartre honouring the lives of their comrades that had been wasted by the cowardice of the generals of the Government of National Defence.

Chapter Five

Shepherdess of Wolves

December. A twelve year old street urchin ran through the mud and slush of the lanes in the rookeries of Belleville. He was bare-footed and wore ragged brown moleskin trousers, a heavy linen shirt and a dark waistcoat. On his head was a large, soft, black beret pushed back on a mass of strong, roughly-cut hair to which it seemed to cling like a dark halo. He carried a bucket of paste and a short broom in one hand. A leather satchel filled with wall posters with a strap too long for him banged at his knee as he ran. He dodged under the belly of a cart-horse blocking the corner of Place Pigalle. He ran past *Le Marmite* and pushed open the door of M. Verdier's press.

"Clement-Thomas has disbanded the Belleville Sharpshooters!"

He pulled a poster out of the bag and held it up in front of the printer.

"You read well enough when it suits you, Dip," said M. Verdier.

"They're plastered all over Belleville."

The boy suddenly sat down on the floor and started crying. The printer stopped the machine and went into the back room. He came back when the boy had calmed down and passed him the jar filled with bonbons.

"Find Mme Lemel and Mlle Michel and tell them," he said.

"Give me your gun," said the boy.

"You'll never get into the *Hôtel de Ville*."

"Give me your gun."

"No," said M. Verdier. He pushed the boy back out onto the street after first checking that the drawer to his desk was still locked. He stood thinking for a minute or two and then unlocked the drawer, took out a revolver and a box of ammunition and hid them under the base-plate of the press.

General Clement-Thomas had commanded the troops that executed his brother after the revolution of 1848. The wall of his printing works still bore the marks of a summary execution. They had dragged the boy out into the street and shot him by the door. Making Clement-Thomas commander of the National Guard was a direct provocation of the northern arrondissements. Now he was quick to blame the failure of the Great Sortie on the citizen soldiers. A story had been put about that the Belleville National Guard were insubordinate and had fled the battlefield. It had enraged the lost children. The bourgeois press took up the slander with a will. It provided Clement-Thomas with an excuse to disband what he knew was the most effective revolutionary force in Paris.

M. Verdier, Nathalie Lemel and Louise Michel met at the press an hour later. By that afternoon they had discovered that the source of the slander was the commander of the Belleville regiment appointed by Clement-Thomas after an arrest warrant had been put out for Gustave Flourens following his attempt to proclaim a commune in the *Hôtel de Ville*. When Flourens arrived on the battlefield in the thick of the fighting the Sharpshooters refused to take orders from the new man, who formally passed command to Flourens before he left and returned to Paris. There he accused them all of insubordination, which was true, and fleeing the fighting, which was not. The revolutionary clubs and the Sharpshooters themselves, quickly organized delegates from other regiments that had witnessed the conduct of the Belleville National Guard who signed a letter to Clement-Thomas repudiating the accusations of cowardice. The disbanded Sharpshooters summoned their own ex-commander to a meeting. He was too nervous to attend, but wrote a letter to the military journal *Combat* retracting his accusations. By late afternoon *Combat* had been published and the progressive press had weighed in on behalf of the Sharpshooters. Lemel, Michel and Verdier composed a wall poster which was running off M. Verdier's press and being got out across Paris by the lost children that evening.

"Some machines work better than guns," said M. Verdier to Dip, passing him a sheaf of posters. "You can shoot the bastard some other time."

The posters raised the spirits of the dispossessed but did little to persuade the bourgeoisie, who were predisposed to believe that the poor were worthless trash. In any case, news of disastrous reversals in the provinces claimed their attention. And the almost complete lack of meat became the main topic of conversation everywhere, even in the *Hôtel de Ville* when the mayors of the arrondissements met with the Government. Any talk of the defence of the city was stifled in case it should raise the issue of arming the people. The Government instead organized daily parades on the Champs Élysées which greatly profited *Le Marmite.* A team of the lost children, organized by Dip, who was a pick-pocket, started to specialize in working the concentrations of wealthy citizens cheering the troops.

The art of picking pockets does not depend on the victim being unaware of the presence of the thief, Dip explained to his selected accomplices in the loft of the House of Lost Children. Neither was it a matter of snatch and run, which was invariably a risky enterprise. The trick was to make your target as aware of your presence as possible while being completely unaware of your motive. One of the kids cried out when Dip stepped back on his foot. Dip was wearing his nailed boots and the other child was in bare feet. He hugged the kid, apologised and took his boots off. Out of one of them he then took a tin bracelet, his victim's prized possession, and handed it back to him.

"See what I mean?" he said. And then:

"You shove them about a bit. Pretend it's an accident. They'll have a go at you just for being there. But they won't notice your hand in their pocket if you make them think of something else. We can work up some different capers. We'll practise here and then try it out on M. Verdier and down the café."

M. Verdier saw them coming. He ignored the kid who stumbled into him and the one who tugged his sleeve and collared Dip.

"You think I was born yesterday?" he said, retrieving his pocket-book.

"Now you lot listen to me. Dip already understands this. We are revolutionaries not thieves. What you expropriate is communal. It already belongs to the workers whose labour has been stolen. And you don't take jewellery. It has to be fenced and fences are crooks no better than the bourgeoisie. Do everything Dip tells you to do. Look out for one another and be careful. You are all valuable citizens. Now I want to talk to Dip alone."

"I'm sorry I showed you up in front of them," he said, "it was sort of like catching a ball, that's all."

To his surprise Dip was not crestfallen.

"I thought you'd guess," he said, and handed M. Verdier his pen.

"You remind me of my brother," said M. Verdier.

Dip's gang did well while the parades lasted, on one occasion bringing back a gentleman's pocket book with a considerable sum in it. The money was used to buy staple foods, which were still to be had at a price with the right contacts. Monelle organised a second gang of children to seek out the children of poor families who would not apply to *Le Marmite* or the clubs because they were supporters of the Church. Flour, oatmeal and the ubiquitous kippers were left on doorsteps where necessary, although some families still threw them out into the street to be eaten by dogs and crows, preferring the blessings of a priest. The Church fed no one. Louise Michel, however, persuaded Georges Clemenceau, who was already supporting the refugee children in her school, to pioneer the provision of some bread in the *Mairie,* and the practise began to spread to other progressive districts in Paris. But the rich craved red meat. Paris began to run out of pet dogs and cats. Horse flesh had soon disappeared. Even the rats, prepared by specialist butchers and euphemistically called "gutter rabbits," began to run out, or became wise. So it was proposed at the highest level to begin slaughtering the animals in the zoo.

The director of the zoo and the newspapers claimed that scarcity of forage necessitated the cull, but it was only a sop to the squeamish. After the more conventional meat, of antelope, zebra and yak had appeared on the shelves of the butchers on the boulevards, kangaroo and camel became available at a price. Finally the two elephants, Castor and Pollux were shot. It was headline news. A special explosive cartridge was designed for a high calibre hunting rifle. Reporters, hunters, zoologists and the curious gentry stood by. The explosive rounds were useless. No one knew where to aim to kill an elephant. The animals slowly bled to death, even after several rounds had been fired into them. The next day their skinned trunks were on sale in the *Boucherie Anglaise* on Boulevard Haussmann at forty francs a pound, enough money to feed eighty poor families for a week.

It had been below freezing for days when the Government announced that another sortie would attempt to break the grip of the Prussians around Paris to the north near Le Bourget.

"We know all that area inside out," said L'Oursin to Mlle Michel when he heard. The lost children had become very familiar with the Prussian lines north of Montmartre. Michel gave the youth some money.

"Go and buy a map. We can mark the Prussian lines on it and I'll give it to Clemenceau to take to the *Hôtel de Ville.*"

In the House of Lost Children the foraging team, L'Oursin and Michel annotated the map along a five kilometre line of trenches and gun emplacements. They made particular reference to a weak part of the Prussian defences close to where they had been captured. Clemenceau took the map to General Trochu himself. He told him the source of the intelligence and mentioned Louise Michel.

"Really?" said Trucho, who had no time for Clemenceau, whom he thought little better than a revolutionary,

"Do you expect me to take an interest in the opinions of a bunch of street Arabs and a hysterical woman?"

He threw the map into his wastepaper bin and dismissed him.

Up in the circus field Monelle found L'Oursin extending the bell of the out-of-tune bass saxophone which he now had on loan from M.Sax, who was building another instrument from scratch. His little hut was warm from the iron stove in which he heated his soldering irons.

"That oaf Trochu chucked the map in his bin and threw Clemenceau out. Called us a bunch of street Arabs!"

To her surprise L'Oursin started laughing. He put the huge instrument on his bed, shut the stove door and started to prepare coffee. She threw off a thick, hooded, ochre-coloured Arab djellaba she had found in the circus's boxes of costumes.

"What's so funny?"

"Well you look the part," he said.

She was furious. Another child was dying in the House of Lost Children and she was hungry and exhausted. *Le Marmite* had reduced its rations to one small meal a day and she was forcing part of her provision on the old perfumer, who was prepared to do without food at all, it seemed, rather than reduce the share of her neighbours. She sat down on the edge of L'Oursin's bed.

"Those shits in the *Hôtel de Ville* are going to march thousands of men onto the Prussian *mitrailleuse's* for nothing."

She was talking about machine-guns. The doctor who had removed the bullet from the lost child's leg after the first of L'Oursin's sorties into no-man's-land had a military background. He talked about the weapon as a distraction while he worked. He knew the deep gouge of a *maitrilleuse* round at a glance. The child recognized the imitation of rapid fire he made, too.

"It's worse than that," said L'Oursin, after a long silence while the coffee percolated, "the ground will be far too hard to dig trenches. Our men are glad they're not going. All Trochu and Ducrot are good for is marching up and down the Champs Élysées. But that's to our advantage, don't you see? They're complete fools. It's good when your enemy is an idiot."

But Monelle, lulled by the warmth and the security of his company, was nodding off. He made room for her on the bed by removing the saxophone and continued working, drinking the coffee himself.

A few days later Monelle pushed the door open to the music room in the school. Michelle was rehearsing some older pupils in a play she had written.

"Come up to the windmills, you can see the army!"

She ran on down to the House of Lost Children, muffled up in the djellaba and skidding on the ice in clogs. There she tipped off Dip's team that there would be sightseers from the boulevards up on the Heights. There was a viewing platform on the top of one of the two windmills that comprised the Moulin de la Galette, but it would be crowded, and Dip would head there, so she went on up to the circus field which had just as good a view.

A crowd had already gathered in the field. The day was still and very cold. The meagre smoke from what fires there remained in the city below rose straight up and then dispersed sideways. To the north the open country was quite clear save where the guns were firing. There patches of dense smoke hung without movement. Since dawn the distant booming of guns could be heard firing along a line that encircled two thirds of the city from the North West to the North East. Crisp, dark lines of troops were clearly visible in the far distance. Nearer by, columns of men, horses and artillery pieces were moving slowly towards the smoke. A telescope had been set up on a tripod. The owner was charging people to view the battle. Even through the telescope it was difficult to see what was happening. In the furthest distance the static lines of men were desperately trying to dig trenches under grapeshot and machine-gun fire. Trochu had already lost the battle, although he was to pour more men towards it all day.

Louise Michel arrived with half a dozen of her older girls and thick-set old man with a battered face who looked like he might once have been a prize-fighter. Monelle recognized Victor Hugo. Hugo saw what he thought was an Arab boy in native costume. He looked in her direction and said *"salam alaikum."* She pushed back the hood of her djellaba, shook hands with Michel and turned to Hugo,

"*Walaikum salam,* M. Hugo", she said, and guessing that he would have heard, as Michel had, of Clemenceau's response from Trochu by now,

"*Les Miserables* is a masterpiece. But you are wrong to believe that society can be reformed. We street Arabs know better."

L'Oursin was astonished at her. Michel pleaded with them to get their instruments, and struggling in the cold with frozen fingers, they entertained the crowd for half an hour. Later Hugo concentrated his considerable charms on her until finally, and just between the two of them, she prodded him in the stomach with her finger and said, with a wink,

"Fuck off fat guts, I'm not selling."

That night the army slept in the open. The ground was too hard to erect tents. Trochu, fearful of the impact on his reputation another defeat would have, kept throwing men at an impregnable enemy firmly dug in. By the third day the troops were on the edge of mutiny. Nine hundred men were frost-bitten. The gun-carriage horses were dying. On Christmas Eve he retreated on Paris. It was only with revolvers in their hands that his officers were able to prevent the troops from shouting for peace as they entered the gates of the city. By the end of the year the temperature had dropped to twelve below zero.

When L'Oursin arrived at the House of Lost Children with an armful of firewood on the first morning of the severe cold there was a great commotion going on. Monelle and the children were trying to get the mule upstairs. The animal was half frozen and dejected. It balked at the climb. L'Oursin rousted out a couple of National Guard from the nearest bar and together they all but carried the miserable creature up into the warmth above. There they tethered it in a corner of the room where it quickly cheered up. They fed it from a sack of oats, expropriated from the army in the Bois de Boulogne. The dogs and cats rearranged themselves suspiciously. Somehow all these animals were being fed. The kids were amazed that the bats did well enough up in the attic, their fur rimed with frost and deep asleep. They quickly woke up and became active when brought down into the warm communal room but soon found their way back up into the attic after a couple of quick laps over the children's heads.

The room was kept warm with a minimum of fuel. The kids had blocked its draughts with rags and paper picked up in the street. The windows had shutters on the outside. They had a small store of firewood and a little coal in the room at street level. For a while now all the coal in the city had been requisitioned by the Government for founding cannon and making gas to fill the balloons that kept the city in contact with the provinces. A little coke was available at a price. But many in the city were beginning to die of the cold, particularly the children and the old. The perfumer moved into the circus master's caravan with him. She laughed at Monelle's surprise. L'Oursin saved fuel by moving into the House of Lost Children. Victor Hugo sent Louise Michel some warm blankets which she immediately gave to her pupils. She slept in an unheated room in her cloak under a single blanket.

After Christmas the Government gave orders to cut down about six square miles of timber in the Bois de Boulogne and the Bois de Vincennes, and to fell hundreds of trees along the boulevards leading out of the city. Depots of firewood were set up. The bourgeois press announced a dole of fuel to the poor. The poor received nothing and now had no trees they could fell themselves as the lost children had been doing for a month. They watched timber being carted out of the depots towards the boulevards.

"Get a poster out for people to apply to the Vigilance Committee or the clubs for a ration of firewood!"

Louise Michel stood in M. Verdier's freezing workshop muffled-up in her cloak with cavalry boots on her feet, her breath frosting as she spoke.

"This place is colder than outside! I'll put you on the list myself."

She went to alert the lost children to get the posters put up across Montmartre and Pigalle, and to tell the National Guard to send representatives to the clubs that night. She hauled L'Oursin out of a bar by his ear and ordered him to organise the lost children and to detail a team of runners. At the Vigilance Committee meeting she raised the roof:

"Am I to watch my pupils die of cold while those fat pigs on the boulevards warm their backsides by a blazing fire?

If they won't distribute the firewood as they promised we must do it ourselves."

She went straight to most rebellious of the clubs and told its best orator to set off a chain reaction of speakers to call for Montmartre to descend on the nearest wood depot at ten o'clock that night. When the woman there grabbed a shawl and put a sword on her hip she knew the matter was settled. At nine thirty the Montmartre drums began to beat. The mob was highly organized. Handcarts were requisitioned without any orders coming down. About a thousand people broke down the gates of the nearest wood depot and the guards fled. By morning the depot was empty and its contents distributed around the clubs. Georges Clemenceau arrived to find a large pile of wood outside the *Mairie* guarded by a couple of National Guard with an encouraging bottle of brandy between them. One of M. Verdier's posters was pinned to the door. That day first Belleville and then other poor districts of Paris rose up too.

The coffin of the second child to die in the House of Lost Children that winter was taken up to the perfumer's house. The ground in the cemetery was frozen to a depth of twenty inches. All over Paris bodies awaited burial. The Montmartre *Mairie* had opened a second mortuary, but the children chose to put the dead child in Monelle's room. There were bats in the old woman's house, and in the Moulin de la Galette, who would surely guard the child. The doctor had no idea what the small boy died of. He simply grew weaker and died without any fuss, surrounded by the other children. He put "poverty" on the death certificate. The

House of Lost Children sank into grief and apathy. So Mlle Michel arrived that evening and told the children the story of her childhood.

"I was born in the Tomb," she began:

"I am a bastard. That means my mother, whom you know, and my father whom you don't, were not married in a church. Most of the workers' children around here are bastards too, so I've come home....."

The children grew restive. What did they care about bastards or of the Church?

"Tell us about the Tomb!"

"The Tomb was what the villagers called our house, which was really a tumble-down chateau. At its corners there were four square towers the same height as the rest of the house. On the south side there were no windows, only loopholes for firing bows or guns out of, so it looked like a castle or a tomb. Everyone called it the Tomb. To the west was a deep forest. When the snow lay thick the wolves would creep from the forest into the Tomb through gaps in the wall and howl in our courtyard. Our dogs would answer them and this concert would last until morning."

At the sound of the word "dogs" one of the dogs around the stove lifted its head from its paws and looked intently at Michel.

"You see! He is loving the story about his ancestors, the free wolves of the forest. After the Revolution all dogs will become wolves again!"

She continued,

"When I took Mme. Eudes there years ago we went deep into the forest where there is a huge druid oak tree and became blood sisters."

Michel took out her knife and mimed cutting her wrist.

"To become blood sisters or brothers you each draw blood like that and then put your wrists together to let your blood mix. I'll show you how to do it properly if you want. When we left the oak the wolves followed us all the way to the edge of the forest. Perhaps they had licked the drops of blood that fell under the tree and become our wolf brothers and sisters because they only looked at us with their big black eyes and did us no harm."

The dog looked up and wagged his tail. Michel winked at him.

"Many animals lived in the Tomb. We had a big Spanish hound with long yellow hair and two sheepdogs. All three dogs answered to the name of Presta. We also had a black and white dog called Médor and a young bitch we named Doe in memory of an old mare named Doe that had died just before we got the bitch. When I gave the mare an apron full of hay her manner would change remarkably. But the thing I remember best about her was stealing my bouquets; she would take them and then lick my face.

When she died my grandfather and I wrapped her head in a white cloth, so no earth would touch it, and buried her outside near our acacia tree.

Michel spoke rapidly, in a quiet voice that suggested she might only now be remembering events long forgotten.

"We had legions of cats too, particularly male ones. We called all our male cats Lion or Darling and all the females Galta. Sometimes the cats crowded us at the fire and my grandfather used the tongs to pick a glowing coal from the fireplace and wave it at them. Then the whole pack ran off.

"My mother my aunt and my grandmothers sat round the table. One read aloud while the others sewed. You know my mother. She's a peasant. She was very beautiful as a girl. The neighbours used to joke and say how could someone so beautiful have an ugly child like me. My grandfather came from the nobility, but he was a republican and a revolutionary. He used the citizen's form of his name. He gave me his name, but now I use my mother's. Names are not important. You can give yourselves any name you want to make up."

Some of the younger children had fallen asleep. A cat had crept onto Michel's lap. L'Oursin kept the stove going.

"In the summer the Tomb filled up with birds that flew in through the broken windows. Swallows came back to their nests of former years; sparrows flew in and out of the windows. Sometimes they flew against the unbroken panes. The larks sang loudly with us. That is, they sang with us when we sang in a major key; when we changed to a minor key they would fall silent. We had partridges, a tortoise, a roebuck, some wild boars, a wolf, barn owls, bats, several broods of orphaned hares that we raised by spoon feeding, a whole menagerie. And of course there was always the colt Zephyr and his grandmother Brouska who was so old no one could remember how old she was. Brouska walked in and out of the rooms in order to take bread and sugar from the hands of people she liked. To those she didn't she showed her long yellow teeth as if she were laughing in their faces. And there were cows, too, the great white Bioné and the young Bella and Néra. I went to their stable to chat with them and they answered me in their own way by looking at me with their soft eyes.

"All these beasts lived on good terms with each other. The cats would lie curled up, following with a negligent eye the birds toddling about on the ground. Even stranger, I never saw a cat bothering about a mouse, and mice lived in all the walls. In the Great Hall, behind the green tapestry that covered the walls, the mice ran around uttering shrill little cries. The mice behaved perfectly, and never gnawed on papers or books and never placed a tooth on the violins, cellos and guitars which were scattered about."

The lost children had heard some of this more than once. They knew better than to interrupt her with questions. She always ended by exhorting them to come to the school.

"In the Tomb there was a library filled with books. All the books of the world. You must come to the school and learn to read! Books will make you free. Like the wolves in the forest. As you are, you are like these poor dogs here that beg for any scraps they can get. Long ago one of my peasant ancestors bought a whole library by the kilogram. Even the peasants read books. I remember his descendants, my uncles, when they were old men. They were tall handsome old men with strong shoulders, powerful judgements and simple hearts. They all had red hair with no silver threads in it, even as old as they were. They had quick minds. They had learned a great mass of information and spoke well. They had old texts, illustrated, with Homer calling down the clouds on his characters; old chronicles from which legends flew so strongly that my great-uncles had adopted some of them; volumes of out-of-date science; novels of bygone days. The women used to read my great-uncle's novels together in the evenings until late into the night. The reader of the evening would lick her thumb to turn the pages while her gentle eyes dropped tears over the misfortunes of the heroes. Some readers read so well that they charmed their listeners and the reading lasted until midnight. Then, still trembling from the impact of the story, some of the women would walk the others back to their homes. The snow spread over everything. The hoarfrost, like flowers in May, covered the branches. The last women, the ones who lived furthest away, ran through the snow to their houses while their friends yelled after them to reassure them." [11]

Of course, the children knew well enough what it was to be read to. Michel herself came and read to them. Monelle and L'Oursin read from a small pile of books on a table in the corner. They knew who Homer was. Monelle was reading The Odyssey to them. But when she spoke of her past Michel cast a powerful spell. She never spoke differently to children from the way she spoke to adults. Much of what she had just said many of them failed to understand. But it gave them a perspective on a strange landscape where Michel strode through the snow and wolves howled in the forest. Perhaps wolves might come to visit their dogs on the night of the Revolution, like the wolves in a book they had seen, but now come out of the forest forever, walking slowly down the mean lanes of Montmartre at midnight.

The stove clicked in the silence. The dogs sighed. They became slowly aware they were hearing another sound. A distant bombardment was underway. The sound of gunfire at night was a new development.

Chapter Six

Snow

In Charleville the guns were not so distant. A mile or two away, on the other side of the Meuse, the town of Mézières was under bombardment. The Rimbaud family were confined to their apartment in the Cours d'Orléans. Arthur Rimbaud was in his room, decorated with the hated, embossed wallpaper that he had been vandalising since he was a child. It was in tatters behind his table leaking plaster dust. He was keeping out of the way of his brother his sister and his mother. It was freezing in there. He was wearing all his old, ragged, travel-stained clothes, the brown bowler hat and fingerless gloves. He was sucking on an empty pipe and reading Baudelaire, the copy of *Les Fleurs du Mal* from Douai that had somehow found its way to Charleville. A pocket-book was open before him at a blank page. Every few seconds the windows rattled with the pressure waves from the gunfire across the river.

While the school was closed, Rimbaud and his friend Ernest Delahaye had spent the warm autumn days together in the parkland called the Bois d'Amour on the Mézières side of the river where Delahaye lived and his parents ran a shop. They read the poems of Hugo. Rimbaud read aloud in a style that had won him school prizes for elocution, occasionally skidding into an Ardennes peasant accent and turning the lines into a scatological parody of romantic verse. Delahaye brought tobacco with him and Rimbaud talked. He talked as if he were possessed. When he launched into a topic his head swam, his inhalations were intoxicating; the air of the Bois seemed to fill his skull with green and golden light. Delahaye listened. He was the negative pole that drew the spark.

They met on the avenue of limes; walked towards one another from the far distance where the trees seemed nearly to meet. A hive of golden leaves clustered on the branches, settled, swarmed out on the ground, crawled in millions along the parallel lines of a highway to nowhere. Rimbaud felt the avenue punch a hole below his heart every time he saw it.

Magic flowers were humming. The slopes cradled him. Fabulously elegant beasts moved about. The clouds were gathered over the high sea. An eternity of warm tears. [12]

He called out to Delahaye,

"Merde, merde, merde! Pepper up your snivels of shit! Find delicate ankhs to rouse your thunders! There! Where the dead girl sinks beneath the high crests! If you have no tobacco I shall eviscerate your guts of violet snot!"

Delahay threw him the tobacco pouch and he lit his pipe. They walked. Rimbaud picked up a stick with which he occasionally whipped the trees.

When the weather grew colder they broke into a gardener's tool-shed to get out of the wind. The place held a couple of old armchairs from which the mice fled when they sat down. Delahaye had brought bread and cheese as well as tobacco and a bottle of wine. Rimbaud drank his half in one go and then collapsed into a chair cackling hysterically. He laughed until he was exhausted. Delahaye gently took the bottle from him and sipped from it while Rimbaud began to talk. Outside it grew dark. They lit a candle. Shadows moved around the narrow space, widening and contracting the walls.

He talked of The Modern, of the city growing like a monstrous leviathan in endless night. Of savage men excavating its veins, weaving the fibres of its nervous system with great hawsers of copper through which the lightning flowed. Underground violet spaces opened and echoed with icy light. Ships strode above the smoke. Crystal boulevards intersected with invisible rails and pulleys. Bridges of the abyss revolved, where the people sang the joy of the new work. Oriflammes of steel flew above the grey unchanging sky, over canals and deserts. How far above or below the acropolis lay the other districts? Here? Where at a word great spaces opened in the firmament, singing voices excavated the hillsides in unknown clefs? Language expanded iron mouths; caves of adamantine vowels; miraculous grammars; prosodies of alchemy. The world was subject to the word!

Delahaye, absorbed in it all, watched a mouse creep and retreat, creep and skitter, and advance by degrees towards the cheese on the workbench.

"Small horseman of the apocalypse," said Arthur Rimbaud sleepily.

A week later he walked into the Bois d'Amour to see the lime trees had been felled. They had been felled outwards and lay, all at the same angle, in two parallel ranks receding into the distance. Beyond them orchards and smallholdings had been obliterated. The landscape was full of people, collecting firewood and arguing. The army were there felling more trees so as to clear sightlines for the artillery being drawn up to oppose any Prussian advance on Charleville should Mézières fall.

In his icy bedroom, staring at the empty page in the notebook, Rimbaud heard the bombardment of Mézières reach its peak late in December. He had not seen Delahaye for a fortnight. After Christmas the gunfire ceased. From the windows of the apartment Prussian soldiers could be seen. His mother gleaned bits of news from neighbours. Mézières had caught fire and lay in ruins. The Delahaye's shop had been destroyed and the family were all dead. In Charleville life was pretty much as usual save for the presence of the Prussian army. The town had surrendered without a fight. On New Year's Day 1871 Arthur was allowed out.

Snow had been falling for days. He went straight to the café on *Place Ducale* where he and Delahaye usually drank. It was full of Prussian soldiers. He stood by the door and slowly filled and lit his pipe. His mother had given him some money at last. The place was unusually noisy. He knew no one there. He stared at the soldiers with his hands in his pockets, puffing at the pipe between his teeth, until the conversation slowed a little. The Prussians saw a ragged child, perhaps a beggar, standing a couple of paces into the bar with the laces of his boots trailing in melting snow. For a moment the boy looked uncertain whether to come any further in. Then he shuffled up to the bar and leaned with his back to it staring round at the soldiers. All eyes were on him now. He produced a coin from his pocket, held it up for all to see, flipped it and slapped it hard on the back of his hand. The slap silenced the last traces of conversation.

"Tails," he said.

And then, over his shoulder to the barman,

"Mein Herr! Giff me ein glass off zee vonderfull Charlefill bier bitte."

He said it through his teeth; the pipe was still clenched between them. There was a long pause. He did not see the barman behind him look from him to the soldiers and begin automatically wiping the counter with his cloth.

"Give me a fucking beer!" he shouted over his shoulder, and then smiled like a cherub into the faces turned in his direction. Someone laughed. The room began to laugh. The boisterous conversation welled up. He turned his back to it and watched the barman fill his glass with a shaky hand.

"I'll tell your mother about this, Arthur," he said.

With a couple of beers inside him Rimbaud walked down to the bridge across the Meuse in heavy snowfall. It was occupied by Prussian soldiers. His shuffling figure came towards them out of the blowing snow. At an order two soldiers crossed bayonets signalling the road ahead was blocked. Rimbaud kept walking. The soldiers had to turn their bayonets towards him to prevent him pushing through. A furious officer shouted

"The way is closed!"

He went so far as to draw his pistol and point it at the ridiculous ragamuffin who stood with his snow-encrusted coat-front touching the points of the bayonets. The officer approached and saw an ill-kempt student with pale, expressionless eyes and a determined mouth. He was under orders to treat French civilians with tolerance; and here was just an angry child.

"Go home," he said quietly.

The boy held his eye with an unnerving stare. He took the pipe from his mouth and pointed with it at the spiralling snow. In the voice of a man twice his weight, an actor's voice that filled the silence, powerful, unnerving, fierce with emotion, he spoke two lines from Doctor Faustus:

"O, I'll leap up to my God! – Who pulls me down?

See, see where Christ's blood streams in the firmament."

It was like a disembodied voice that came from somewhere above or behind the strange little figure and was invoked by it out of the spirals of snow. It was so loud and so unexpected it made the skin on the officer's neck creep. He stepped back.

Rimbaud turned on his heel and walked back the way he had come, his form slowly disintegrating into the falling snow.

A couple of days later the cordon round Mézières was lifted. Rimbaud walked in the early morning to a vantage point from which he could see the town still burning. The bridge was unguarded. The snow had stopped. A single set of tracks crossed over the bridge through ankle-deep snow. He trudged across, placing his feet in the other footprints, trying to keep the snow out of his boots. Half way over he crouched and laced them up. He followed the tracks along the avenue of fallen limes and up through the shattered orchards where the broken branches reached out of the snow like hands. There was a strange smell, half animal, half mineral. Over the rise, the ruins of Mézières were black and red and veined with white, smoking, and in places still lapped with flames. There was no one else to be seen. He walked into the stricken town feeling strangely elated. He realized that he was looking into the future. Houses had been torn in two, one side collapsed into the street, the other revealing dolls house rooms, a bed, a mirror on the wall, floor joists resting on nothing, trailing wallpaper - bourgeois respectability cracked open like an egg.

In the cities, the mud suddenly appeared to me red and black, like a mirror when the lamp moves around in the next room, like a treasure in the forest! Good luck, I cried, and saw a sea of flames and smoke in the sky, and, to left and to right, all riches blazing like a billion thunders.

In the town centre the law courts, the prison and the police station were all untouched, but the offices of a radical newspaper, the *Progrès des Ardennes,* to which he had submitted pieces, had received a direct hit. In that wordless state of mind prior to thought he understood fully that it is order, and not disorder, that always presides over chaos.

There was so much destruction in the street where the Delahaye's shop was that it was difficult to know where it had been. He came upon two drunk Prussian soldiers picking over some damaged merchandise. They were the first people he had seen that morning. With a shock he realized they were standing on the ruins of the shop. They ignored him. He stumbled up onto the pile of rubble, staggered and put his hand on one man's shoulder to steady himself, saying, ridiculously, "I beg your pardon," and began pulling away the broken masonry and split timbers where he saw stone stairs leading down to the cellar. The soldiers started to help him when they heard some sounds down there. It took a while to reach the top of the door and kick it in. With a sudden terrible screaming two cats sprang out, covered in masonry dust. One of them ran up Rimbaud's leg and leapt off his shoulder.

Ernest Delahaye, who had been alerted that the shop was being looted, saw his friend laughing hysterically on top of the ruins of his family's business in the company of two Prussian soldiers.

"Oh, hello Ernest," said Arthur.

"Look, I've brought you the Baudelaire to read."

And he pulled out of his pocket Izambard's first edition copy of *Les Fleurs du Mal.*

****

At just that moment, L'Oursin was drinking red wine from a bottle with some National Guard who were at the cannon on the Buttes du Montmartre. An alto saxophone hung from its sling around his neck. The men were gasping for air after vigorously dancing lewd waltzes with one another in the snow. Two women, who had come with food for them from *Le Marmite,* were laughing. L'Oursin passed them the bottle.

The cannon on the Buttes were lined up on two wide terraces cut into the hill on its steepest side just below the summit. That side of the Heights looked east over the city, and had been quarried and delved into for centuries. The Buttes surmounted a chaotic wasteland, bare of trees that rose above the cluttered roofs of Pigalle and was exposed to the coldest winds. There was a derelict stone building nearby in which the National Guard could take shelter and a cellar beneath the ruins of another where the shot and powder were stored. Snow had drifted against the windward cannon almost burying some of them, but their ordered lines, two ranks of fifteen guns each gave the place some slight resemblance to a normal military post. The same could not be said of the men. They took a pride in wearing the scruffiest arrangements of bits of uniform and old clothes. Some of these men had been present at the battle of the Marne and had been given new kit. But what they had been issued were items rejected by the regular army units, of poor making and in odd tones of blue, such had been the rush to equip troops for the sortie. The wrong colour of this stuff was felt to be an insult, and the National Guard units had been mocked for it by the troops of the regular army, so most of the issue was passed on to poor families where the material had been unpicked to make warm clothes for children and the elderly. The men on the Buttes were a ragged lot. They preserved their boots by wrapping their feet in sacking bound up with string. They were a wide range of ages, too; some were men in their fifties. There were no discernible higher ranks. Their battalion commander was Louise Michel's friend, the Blanquist revolutionary Émile Eudes. The Montmartre National Guard drew their pay from the *Mairie* each week and defended the interests of their community. Decisions were made after general discussion around the fire in one of the shelters while passing a bottle. But they were competent. Some of the older men had experience of former wars and a revolution in 1848. Their store of shot and powder was properly maintained and guarded. Their Chassepot rifles were new and not at all second-rate like the uniforms. Many of the artillery pieces were newly founded and had been bought by subscription from people scarcely able to feed themselves. Their muzzles and breech-vents were sealed with oil-cloth and the elevation screws and mounting trunnions properly greased. They were no less ready for use for a bit of snow.

L'Oursin and the National Guard took shelter in the derelict house. The sound of distant gunfire was now more or less continuous. The two women had put a big pot of vegetable stew on the edge of the fire but only one loaf of bread on the table, where there were a dozen bottles of wine.

"Franck's back home," said one of the men. "Says the Krauts blew his fucking pants off in Avron."

"Pity they didn't blow his balls off," said another.

"He's deserted."

Franck, who was known them all, had enlisted in one of the Parisian battalions of the regular army. He had a large family and needed the money. His children were being educated at Michel's school free of charge. He was a mechanic. The siege had put him out of work but his skills made him valuable to a gunnery unit. His partner was active in the clubs and they were members of the *Le Marmite* food cooperative.

"I saw his woman and the kids down in *Le Marmite* just now," said L'Oursin, "She said he was ready to shoot Trochu next time he came in range, so he thought it was time to get out of it."

During the Prussian advance across the plain of Avron east of Paris the French troops had come under the heaviest artillery bombardment yet experienced by any army. The embankments and trenches were brittle as glass and blew into a shower of fragmented, frozen earth like grape-shot when hit. There followed a terrible retreat under fire hauling cannon back into the city.

"He says he's coming up here tomorrow and fuck the pay," said the first man.

"We'll find him some kit," said another.

A third, who was actually the sergeant, said,

"Let's have a whip round and I'll see if I can get some pay sorted out down the *Mairie;* Slug down there needs some cash for medicine for the kid anyway."

Small coin began silently dinting the ash at the edge of the fire where the sergeant was ladling out soup.

"I'll ask Mme Lemel for a donation," said L'Oursin, wiped his bowl clean with some wet sacking, put the saxophone in its case, and stepped out into the blowing snow.

In the meeting room above the café Nathalie Lemel put twenty francs in L'Oursin's hand, enough on its own to bribe the official at the *Mairie.* But she insisted it was not to be thought of as bribery.

"Slug's wife never told me she was desperate for medicine," she said, "I'll make sure she gets it. This is not a bribe. It's just helping two families out with the same money. If they catch Franck they could shoot him." L'Oursin knew this as well as she did, but she felt it necessary to make her position clear. She thought the deal was sailing a bit close to the wind. "Come to think of it, I'll take the money to Slug's wife myself and have a word with him on the way back. He'll do what I say and help Franck, out of good will. Tell the sergeant to bring the cash he's collected down here. If he spends it on booze thinking the whole thing has been sorted out I'll brain him. I don't know why you are looking at me like that, L'Oursin. Give me that money back and go and play your saxophone somewhere." Desertion and defrauding the state were not moral considerations for Nathalie Lemel.

Before he went back to the Buttes, L'Oursin dropped into the House of Lost Children to leave his saxophone there. Three terrified new children had arrived. The Prussians had started bombarding Paris itself. Their house in a poor district south of the river had collapsed after being hit by an explosive shell. Miraculously they all survived. They had been dug out of the ruins after some hours. Their mother was dead. The neighbours knew of no relatives; she had been a refugee from the provinces. A delegate to the Central Committee had brought them to *Le Marmite* when he came to the meeting of the Committee there. They were between five and eight years old. Monelle put a bucket of water on the stove to heat; a blanket was hung in front of a tin bath in one corner of the room and they were washed. They were covered with plaster dust and soot. Now they were wrapped in clean blankets until fresh clothes could be found. L'Oursin got the sax out and played softly, which seemed to ease their fears a little. Food arrived from the café. The doctor was sent for. Three older children were appointed to care for one child each. After an hour or so they looked well enough until you looked into their eyes.

L'Oursin looked in on M. Verdier in the print shop after things had settled down in the House. The hand-cranked cylinder press had a big roll of red paper in it. Red posters were drying on lines in the back of the shop.

"L'Oursin! Get on the guillotine!"

He spent the rest of the day cutting up posters as they rolled off the press.

To the people of Paris.

Delegates from twenty arrondissements of Paris.

The government, on September 4, was responsible for the national defence. Has it fulfilled its mission?

No !

By their procrastination, their indecision, their inertia, those who govern us have led us to the brink of the abyss. They have known neither how to administer nor how to fight. We die of cold, almost of hunger. Sorties without object, deadly struggles without results, repeated failures. The Government has given the measure of its capacities; it is killing us. The perpetuation of this regime means capitulation. The politics, the strategies, the administration of the Empire by the men of the 4th of September have been judged. Make way for the people! Make way for the Commune!

The Red Poster anticipated a surge of dissatisfaction with the Government felt even on the boulevards. The Prussians were soon firing hundreds of shells into the city every night. A shell exploded in the Luxembourg Gardens, tearing up the trees. The Prussian gunners appeared to be targeting churches and hospitals. The bombardment was most intense in the medieval quarter south of the river, one of the poorest districts in Paris, where the three new lost children came from. Families fled north to the right bank, braving the intense cold as the Seine started to freeze outwards from its banks. A shell struck the Montmartre cemetery shattering tombs. Monelle and the lost children cleared the grave of the dead child of marble fragments and rubble and swept the snow from it. Night after night the clubs called for a revolution to clear the way for the proper conduct of the war by all the people of Paris The Prussians were 200,000 against a potential force of 500,000 in Paris if the National Guard were included.

Much of this force, particularly in the poor quarters, had always had more loyalty to the community and class it was drawn from than to the state. National Guard battalions were now in contact with one another through the vigilance committees of the twenty arrondissements. The vigilance committees, which were the voice of revolutionary republicanism, sent delegates to the Central Committee. These were men of the middle sort, ranging from articulate revolutionary workers and artisans to the small bourgeoisie, like M. Verdier, and radical republicans who had spent time in prison or in exile for their part in the struggle against the Empire. They had ideologies that ranged from liberal republican to anarchist and communist. But first they were democrats. The Mayors, who were the putative representatives of the Paris citizenry, at least so far as the bourgeoisie were concerned, had been appointed by the Government of National Defence, and many were the same men who had been in post under Louis Napoleon. They were not elected, and the Government of National Defence had no mandate either. Conservative and monarchist politicians, who represented the interests of property, the Church and the military command, had assumed power after the mob had forced a return to the Republic, and the liberal left had been too disunited to step in. Now the Central Committee was quietly organizing a way to hold municipal, or *commune,* elections in Paris. And for many the word *Commune* meant more than simple municipality; it meant real democracy, power in the hands of the people.

In the *Hôtel de Ville* the gouty martinets of the regular army saw nothing but barbarism in the people of Paris. Since the uprising of the 31st they conceived an implacable hatred of the National Guard. Trochu preened himself as the defender of civilization against atheism and disorder. This was the same civilization, of course, that Bismarck defended. It was said that the Church held Trochu and Trochu held Paris. Instead of amalgamating the forces of the city in unity, of giving to all the same *cadres,* the same uniforms, the same flag, the name of National Guard, Trochu had maintained the three divisions: the regular army, the mobiles of the provinces and the civilian National Guard. The army, incited by the staff, shared the Blimps' hatred of the Paris *canaille.* The mobiles, prompted by their officers, who were the cream of the country squires, blamed their privations on the people of Paris and its National Guard. Trochu was acting as the midwife to a civil war.

Louise Michel, skidding down the icy road from the Buttes that passed the Moulin de la Galette, ran into Monelle, who was returning from visiting the perfumer and the circus master. Michel looked remarkably well for a woman in her forties who ate little and worked tirelessly. Her eyes shone and her complexion was warmed with exercise.

"Those jack-asses in the *Hôtel de Ville* have finally voted for another sortie!"

She took Monelle by the shoulders and kissed her on both cheeks. The windmill above them looked black and menacing against the white snow-sky. The tamarisk trees in the garden were weighed down with snow.

"I just spoke with Hugo. Neither Trochu nor Ducrot think it will succeed but they are terrified the small owners will combine with the *canaille* before they can capitulate to the Prussians. Even the pigs down on the boulevards are calling the Government the band of Judas. The Master says they are planning to throw the citizens against Bismarck. Vinoy thinks it can succeed, but Hugo says it's a conspiracy to destroy us. He says that negotiations for capitulation are nearly complete. I just went up to tell the men at the guns. Heroes all! They are itching for a fight! The reactionaries are fools to underestimate the people. We'll spit and roast Bismarck and then turn on them!"

Monelle looked at the older woman. Her rage was like a fire that warmed everyone it touched.

"I'm going up to see poor Jacques," she said. "Come with me Louise."

They sank up above their knees in the drifted snow piled up against the perfumer's door in the house behind the mill, and climbed the creaking stairs. The frozen corpse of the lost child was in a coffin resting on trestles in Monelle's room. The window was open to keep the room as cold as possible and snow had blown in and piled up on her table. They slid aside the coffin lid. Monelle touched the icy face. He looked as if sculpted from polished grey stone. She blew on her fingers, picked up a guitar and, sitting on her bed, played a Breton lullaby taught to her by Nathalie Lemel. Michel stood, tall and silent, looking out of the open window at the snow beginning to fall again. She was making a spell to call up the wolves of Haut Marne.

Chapter Seven

Betrayal

Franck, although he did not know it yet, was officially listed as lost in action. His comrades had been quick to defend his interests when he went missing and questions were asked. His commanding officer smelled a rat but said nothing. Parisian units of the regular army were close to mutiny. Slug arranged for him to take the pay of a National Guardsman who really was dead. This meant that the dead man's pay, which had been finding its way to Louise Michel to help feed the refugees in her school, would now help keep Franck's family fed. Neither Franck nor his partner were very happy about this, but Michel told them that Hugo had offered to cover the shortfall and more.

By mid-January the snow had thawed. It took a further week for the ground to unfreeze. Monelle broke off the long icicles that had grown on the Moulin de la Galette and packed little Jacques' coffin with them. She had been instructed by the circus master, who knew most things. The child was buried, still partly frozen, in the same grave as the other lost child. Melting ice-water poured through the floor of Monelle's room into the perfumery below, but no one worried about that. L'Oursin brought some wood and lit a fire.

In the *Hôtel de Ville* they talked of silencing the complaints of the rabble for good with the sound of the guns. For the sortie Trochu produced only 85,000 men. Half of them were National Guard: old men and their sons, partly-trained. The entire army was supported by only 150 artillery pieces. They marched beneath the Arc de Triomphe and out along Haussmann's avenue, now bare of trees, towards Neuilly Bridge. They were cheered by the *canaille* as they marched. Lovers, wives and partners helped to carry their rifles and kit. An improvised baggage train of cabs, removal vans and omnibuses had been thrown together. The *canaille* roared. Children ran among the ranks or held their fathers' hands. Their passing seemed for a few hours to unify the classes in Paris. The Bourgeoisie, watching the procession from their balconies along the *Avenue de la Grande Armée*, were moved. The reactionary press gushed. Everyone loves the dispossessed when they are on their way to die. And the passion and commitment of the National Guard, at last sent in regimental numbers into battle, was palpable. For a day Paris believed it would be free.

Franck, the sergeant and the men of the Montmartre gun-crew were among them. They were placed in an infantry battalion. Trochu forced the National Guard regiments to spend the night in the muddy fields below the fort at Mt. Valérien. They formed the left flank and most of the centre, commanded by General Vinoy, one of the more capable generals in Paris. Behind them the other regiments were bogged down at the bottle-neck at Neuilly Bridge. They were not in place by morning, and the right flank, commanded by Ducrot was not in place by noon. The National Guard, watched by Trochu from the terrace of Mt. Valérien, fought, as Vinoy later admitted "with the impulse of old troops." They took all the positions assigned to them, advancing on Versailles, where Bismarck had the confidence to crown himself Emperor of Germany in the Hall of Mirrors two nights previously. Ducrot failed to advance. Vinoy neglected to put artillery on the heights that had been stormed by the National Guard. In all only thirty pieces were in place along the whole line. The Prussians were allowed to sweep the crests at their ease and at four o'clock sent out assault columns. The National Guard gave way and then firmed up, checking the advance. All but Franck and the sergeant of the Buttes gun-crew were killed in this test of strength at Buzenval. Towards six o'clock, when the Prussian fire had diminished, Trochu ordered a retreat. The generals, who had scarcely deigned to visit the National Guard, declared they could not hold out a second night. Battalions returned weeping with rage. There were 40,000 reserves between Mt. Valérien and Buzenval that were never put into the battle.

After dark, during the retreat, Trochu and his staff passed the column of National Guard infantry that Franck and the sergeant were in. The commander-in-chief gave the troops a wide berth, but Franck recognized the white plumes of his rank. He left the column quietly, and once out of sight, aimed his Chassepot at Trochu and fired. At the last moment Trochu's horse nodded and the bullet missed him, hitting an Orderly Officer in the chest and passing right through him. The men in the column started yelling

"Prussians! Prussians!" and hundreds of rounds were loosed off against the fleeing Staff. No one noticed Franck's act of mutiny. He never told the sergeant.

Franck and the sergeant lay in the mud all night waiting to re-cross Neuilly Bridge into Paris. The army was without tents. Trochu delayed them until noon, in pouring rain, until marching-bands could be got up to give the population of Paris the impression that this was not a rout. But the *Avenue de la Grande Armée* was lined with shocked and sullen people. Women and children, desperate for news, invaded the ranks. The balconies above them were empty now. Four thousand men, mostly from the ranks of the National Guard, died at Buzenval.

The *Le Marmite* café and the street outside filled with angry people. By evening the clubs were overflowing with families and with National Guardsmen too enraged to sleep. In the café some lay under the tables, in full kit, muddy and soaked. By midnight the survivors were got home. The wet streets emptied out. It seemed unnaturally silent when Monelle and L'Oursin returned to the House of Lost Children.

It was the National Guard of Belleville and Montmartre, this time, and not the *canaille* who presented themselves in arms before the gates of Mazas prison. They demanded the release of Gustave Flourens. Faced with a battalion with fixed bayonets, the Governor did as he was told.

"It's mutiny," said M. Verdier to Dip and L'Oursin, in the steamy café. "And not before time."

He carefully divided his ration of one salt herring and a hunk of bread between them. He poured three glasses of red wine. No one complained if M. Verdier drank his own wine in the café.

"We are organizing delegates from all the regiments to a proposed Central Committee of the National Guard," he went on. "Essentially we are forming an alternative state. We are laying the foundations of it. We have built a structure for holding proper elections when needed. The battle for Paris is lost. The Bourgeoisie will capitulate now. How that will all play out is anyone's guess."

"We ought to descend on the *Hôtel de Ville* now," said Dip.

"They have the provincial army at their backs," said M.Verdier. "Even if we did succeed, which is very unlikely, we would only inherit the blame for the Prussian victory. Let them stew in their own juice. We bide our time. We build structures. We build our own army. Nothing can stop Bismarck now. But he has his own workers to fear at home. Bismarck won't stay long in France."

"So we give him Alsace?" L'Oursin looked up at the printer.

"What do we care about kingdoms and thrones? German workers are our brothers!" L'Oursin and Dip remembered the Prussian soldier who set them free and knew it was true.

Tactical considerations meant nothing to Louise Michel. Haunted by the wolves, druids, and the Gallic ancestors of Haute Marne, she shared the romantic nationalism of Victor Hugo. And she was uncontrollable. Spontaneity, inspiration, possession, were as powerful forces in her actions as they were in her poetry. Everything she did or said was an expression of freedom. Louise Michel did not wait for the world to be free. She lived in complete freedom in the present; and never more so than when faced with oppression. Oppression and the threat of violence were the doors that opened onto her liberty. She sought danger like a lover. It intoxicated her.

Her rhetoric blew like a fierce wind in the clubs. It gave new life to the cold, hungry and miserable dispossessed of Montmartre. When Trochu resigned after the disaster of Buzenval her contempt was icy. She had intimate knowledge of the intrigues in the *Hôtel de Ville* from Hugo, who was party to everything that went on there. She told how those who longed for surrender had thrown themselves into attitudes. How the lily-livered mayors even affected to fly into a passion and Trochu had demonstrated very philosophically to them the need to negotiate with the enemy. But he would have nothing to do with it. He tendered his resignation, insinuating that they should surrender in his stead. She told how they cut wry faces, protested, still imagined they were not responsible for this issue; how all the generals unanimously decided that another sortie was impossible; how they blustered and postured, seeking to cheat history into the belief that they had to the last resisted capitulation; how the discussion grew heated. At 3.00 a.m. news came in that Flourens had been released by a mutinous citizen guard. The Government hastened to elect Vinoy in Trochu's place. His first act was to arm against Paris, to dismantle the outer defences against the Prussians, to recall the troops of Suresne, Gentilly, Les Lilas and to call out the cavalry and gendarmerie. She told them that a battalion of mobiles had now fortified themselves in the *Hôtel de Ville,* and that Clement-Thomas was to issue a furious proclamation: "The *canaille* is joining the enemy!"

The *canaille* in the clubs hooted with derision. Plans were made to hold a demonstration in front of the *Hôtel de Ville* the next day, a Sunday. L'Oursin, Monelle and half a dozen of the lost children, including Dip, persuaded M. Verdier to come with them. He produced a tattered red flag from the back of the shop.

"We flew it over the barricades in'48," he said. He was smiling. M. Verdier was not in the habit of running with the *canaille,* but the Central Committee were confident it would be a demonstration only. Rigault, the police commissioner for the northern arrondissements, old M. Blanqui and other respected republicans, perhaps Hugo himself, would attend to show support for an almost universal demand to continue with the Parisian defiance of Bismarck.

The circus master, L'Oursin and Monelle walked with the contingent from *Le Marmite.* It was Sunday, the sun shone. The circus master and Monelle were in commedia dell'arte costumes and heavy make-up as Pantalone (the money-bags) and La Signora (his unfaithful wife). L'Oursin wore his bandsman's uniform and took along the great bass saxophone. They would entertain the crowd, starved of colour and laughter, by acting impromptu scenes from the lives of the Bourgeoisie.

By mid-day there were five thousand people in *Place de l'Hôtel de Ville*. The three circus entertainers wove a path of chaos and delight through the crowd. The bass saxophone boomed and roared. Pantalone beat his wife who escaped and discovered Raol Rigault, already a little drunk, and threw herself upon him. Pantalone, in a red body- stocking, a blue cloak and wearing a red carnival-mask with an enormous beak of a nose, made to beat both of them with his stick. Old M. Blanqui himself, who was nearby, edged away and took refuge in a bar on the corner of a side street where he was joined by M. Verdier and the red flag of '48. He bore too striking a resemblance to Pantalone, perhaps. Louise Michel arrived, drawn to the baying of the saxophone. Pantalone made to beat her in an ecstasy of passion. He withdrew when she seized his stick and weighed into him, none too gently, while La Signora, with her foot-high pile of silver ringlets and wide-hipped skirt, screamed horribly enough to raise the hair of those nearby.

This fiery kernel of disorder, that seemed to stir through the crowd like a small whirlpool, was quite audible and visible from the *Hôtel de Ville*. There had appeared at its windows the forms of Breton Mobiles to whom the crowd called and waved. A deputation from the demonstration was received with insults at mid-afternoon by an official non-entity. Shortly afterwards the 101st battalion of the National

Guard arrived from the Left Bank shouting "Death to the traitors!" It poured into the mass of people like a dark river. At the same time, from the north, the 207th arrived from the Batignolles, having marched down the boulevards and linked up with battalions from Montmartre and Belleville. It debouched from Rue de Temple, with a band and drummers at its head, and drew up in proper order before the *Hôtel de Ville.* The stocks of its rifles were uppermost as a sign of peaceful intent. Red flags flew. There were calls for *Commune.* The singing of the Marseillaise became local and then general, led at first by L'Oursin and then taken up by the band. After an hour the National Guard withdrew and the troops dispersed. Most returned home, but a few mingled with the crowd, by now augmented with sightseers.

L'Oursin, Monelle and the circus master played out scenes in a ring that opened in the heart of the crowd. Suddenly the saxophone was torn from L'Oursin's mouth. He nearly went over. No one was near him, but he heard a simultaneous crack and then a pattering sound nearby and the sound of rifle-fire further away. People were screaming and running in all directions. From the windows of the *Hôtel de Ville* the Breton Mobiles were pouring volleys into the crowd. L'Oursin, Monelle and the Master ran for the side street where Blanqui and M.Verdier had started up from their table. They could see some National Guard returning fire from behind lamp posts and from the corners of the streets that led to the square, which had rapidly emptied save for half a dozen prone figures. In the centre, one person stood facing the *Hôtel de Ville.* Louise Michel was methodically firing her revolver in the direction of the

Mobiles at the windows. She could hear a sound that reminded her of summer hail in Vroncourt. Bullets from the Mobiles were hitting the ground all around her. None touched her. Nothing would ever touch Louise Michel. When she had emptied the revolver she stooped to look at the woman lying at her side. She was dead, shot through the neck, and with, thought Michel, an extraordinary quantity of blood beside her. She refilled the revolver from the apron pocket of her dress and continued firing. She was accurate enough, she noticed with amusement, to clear the windows she aimed at for a moment. She felt exultant, like she did when she roused an audience. She loved the sons of Gaul firing at her. They were wrong-headed but true heroes! Soon they would fight for revolution too. When the revolver was empty she shouted "You brigands!" at them and walked calmly away towards the street where she could see Monelle's tall head-dress in the crowd. All the lost children where there.

L'Oursin was bleeding from a gash to the side of his jaw where a bullet had touched him before hitting the saxophone where the upper part of its coiled tubing stood higher than his head when he played. He sat at a table, drinking from a bottle of wine and looked with dismay at the instrument. He tried to think how he could repair it. He dabbed at his cheek with the red flag of '48 that M.Verdier had passed to him. The bullet had gone right through the tube, which he thought could probably be straightened, beaten cylindrical again and patched on both sides. Michel was talking to Raoul Rigault, who was covered in the blood of a friend who had been killed at his side. A cry went up from the National Guards who were firing from the corner of the street. A second unit of Mobiles was entering the far side of the square. The guards continued firing while they all made a safe escape.

The next day L'Oursin took the saxophone to M. Sax at his workshop on the Left Bank. He had half a dozen herrings, a small quantity of pork and a loaf of dark bread with him. *Le Marmite* had been helping to feed M.Sax, who at the time was almost bankrupted by legal costs incurred while fighting for the copyright of his invention. L'Oursin told Mme Lemel that if they wanted saxophone music in Montmartre the only person who knew how to maintain the instruments should be fed.

For some while M. Sax had been sleeping in his workshop, to save fuel to heat soldering-irons so that he could continue with his work. L'Oursin was surprised that Sax was so delighted to see him, even with his bass saxophone in such a state. He told the youth that he had been present in the *Place de l'Hôtel de Ville* just in time to hear bullets whistling past his ears. Sax, if he thought about politics at all, was a monarchist and a bourgeois by instinct. But there is nothing like a near miss from a bullet, and the sight of people you have just been talking to shot down by the defenders of bourgeois civilization and order to produce a change in political attitude. He had gone for a walk and been shot at for it. He had remained loyally in Paris throughout the siege and not fled to Belgium. Now the same people who were about to capitulate to Bismarck, and make *his* country more vulnerable to the Prussian beast, were trying to kill him; he, Adolphe Sax, who had invented the instrument that made French military bands the envy of the world, who had seen the product of his genius stolen by these same French who now aimed bullets at his heart. M.Sax was not sure quite sure whom he hated, or why, but he was turned a revolutionary overnight; a *Communard.*

"You can start by paying your subscriptions to the *Le Marmite* cooperative back to October," said L'Oursin quietly, so as not to disturb Sax who was beginning to disassemble the instrument. "Let it be your first revolutionary act," and then, noticing a stiffening in the shoulders of the instrument-maker,

"I think we may be able to get hold of some 1.5 mm sheet brass for you. We have a big network."

He sat down and looked over some drawings M. Sax was making for a massive, sub-contrabass saxophone that descended in pitch to the frequency of the deepest organ stop. M. Sax was uncontrollable in his own way, he thought, and good material for a revolutionary. He prepared some food for the Master and then tidied up the workshop while Sax removed both the bell and the damaged upper bow of the instrument and replaced them with parts he had in stock.

In the House of Lost Children Monelle was finding it difficult to talk sense into the more fiery spirits. On the Monday after the demonstration a group of them, led by Dip, had returned to the *Hôtel de Ville* to shout insults at the Breton Guard there and to throw filth at them.

"I'm up yer mother's arse, you fuckers!" shouted Dip, shying balls of horse dung over the railings behind which the Mobile guards stood. A volley of shit from the other kids caused the guards to break ranks. One of them took a pot shot at Dip which zipped past his ear. Some people crossing the square scattered. An officer started shouting hysterically. The kids ran round to the unguarded side of the building, their pockets filled with stones, and broke three windows as they ran. In one of the rooms that were hit, Jules Favre, the leader of the bourgeois republicans in the Government of National Defence, was talking to the Mayors. Shards of glass showered the assembly which was sitting around a grand table. They were already alarmed by the sound of gunfire near the building. Then a half-brick hit one of the mayors. A couple of them dived under the table when they heard a closer shot fired at the heels of the children who were just then vanishing into the warren of medieval alleys which the great building had shouldered aside. It was a turning point that silenced the last feigned opposition from the Mayors. It was decided that Favre should go to Versailles to seek a settlement with Bismarck after they had all regrouped into a safer room. It would have happened sooner or later in any case, but the lost children had a greater influence on the course of history in that moment than any of the august politicians present.

An order went out to close the clubs. It was met with derision in the working-class arrondissements. An order went out to disarm all but the tame National Guard units in the wealthy districts. This too was unenforceable. Radical newspapers were shut down with greater success. M.

Verdier laughed when Dip, who had been scouring the boulevards for government wall-posters, brought him the news.

"They're panicking," he said, "and I think you must be to blame!"

Hugo had been quick to inform Michel of the unfortunate scenes in the *Hôtel de Ville* the previous day. Meanwhile M. Verdier was running off hundreds of wall posters, as detailed as pages of a newspaper, which Dip and his team were getting up all over Paris by delegating work out to a network of kids co-ordinated through the emerging Central Committee of the National Guard. The news of the decision to send Favre to Versailles was out the next day.

It was for this reason that two days later Jules Favre, who always affected to be photographed with one hand in his coat like Napoleon, shaved off his august beard, cropped his hair and borrowed the clothes of a coachman. Thus disguised, for fear the National Guard who patrolled the boulevards leading west out of Paris should recognize him, he sat beside the driver of a cab, muffled up, during a late-night journey to the river south of Neuilly. There, he and a small party from the *Hôtel de Ville,* crossed the inky Seine through the floating ice in a boat so full of bullet holes they had to bail it out with their boots. They were met on the other side by a Prussian cavalry detachment, given horses, and shivering in their wet stockings escorted to Versailles to parley with Bismarck over the fate of France.

The bombardment of Paris ceased abruptly the next day. Louise Michel prowled around M. Verdier's printing shop white with fury.

"Those weak-headed shits have sold France down the river!" she shouted.

She and Verdier were having a row. Dip sat in a corner and marvelled at the folly of adults.

"I don't give a toss, Louise, and neither should you. What's the difference between a French exploiter of the people and a German one? Nothing! We fight for our class. I don't give a fig for France!"

"Class! Class! What is class? There are suffering people and those demons who make them suffer. Class! My grandfather was a nobleman and I am a bastard," she shouted. And then, furious,

"A French bastard!"

Dip started to laugh. He tried to stifle it. He was snorting behind the roller press. M. Verdier tried to resist but his lips were twitching under the savage stare of his friend. Suddenly Michel collapsed into laughter too. She threw a handful of posters over Verdier's head.

"We are all French bastards," said Verdier at last. "You fight for the French. I'll fight for the bastards."

In the House of Lost Children Monelle and the kids were listening to the silence. The mule and the dogs were listening too. The mule sighed, knelt down and collapsed contentedly on his side. His coat had been combed until it shone and his hooves were polished with blacking. No one said anything. Monelle got the guitar and sang *Le Temps des Cerises.*

"And lovers will have the sun in their hearts."

The next day the Government of National Defence published the basis of the negotiations. There would be a two week armistice. The forts around Paris would surrender. All soldiers and mobiles were to be disarmed except for one division. Four hundred thousand men had surrendered to two hundred thousand for fear that a democratic municipal assembly, elected by the poor as well as the rich, might govern Paris. Bismarck's greatest concern during the talks was that he could inherit a democracy. German flags appeared on all the forts. Not content with surrendering Paris, Favre in effect surrendered France. The National Government in Bordeaux had not been informed of the proposed negotiations. Now the army that had invested Paris was free to turn against the rest of France. The largest remaining French force threw itself into Switzerland on a feint from the Prussians. Bismarck imposed a 200,000,000 franc indemnity on Paris to be paid in a fortnight. The armistice was imposed on all the armies in the country. The humiliation of France was complete.

Favre boasted that he had saved the arms of the National Guard, but Bismarck knew that to take these it would have been necessary to storm Paris. The resupply of the city commenced. A kind of guilty horror hung over the silent boulevards, noticed by the lost children, who raced down to *Les Halles* where there was chaos and plenty within a few days. The mule was got downstairs as soon as the first food arrived in Paris, harnessed to a cart and taken to *Les Halles,* where Mme Lemel and Monelle shouldered the servants of the wealthy aside and drove hard bargains with the merchants. They were aided by Dip and his team. Cries of theft went up. Amid the jostling and the chases, Lemel, smoking a cigar, remained focussed and calm. The cart was soon loaded. It left in its wake a curious, dizzy calm.

The International Working Men's Association combined with the Central Committee of the Twenty Arrondissements to put forward nominations to run for office in the new French Assembly which was to be elected as a condition of the deal with Bismarck. The poll was to be held within a week and would certainly produce the election of monarchists, churchmen and conservatives; possibly even the return to a monarchy. In the clubs the dispossessed put up their own nominations. These they communicated to the Central Committee. Only Paris put forward progressive candidates, among them Garibaldi. Across France, the Church the squires and the monarchists, the dead hand of reaction, prepared to take over. They would inherit the power of Empire. The Church and the Rurals had fifty years anger at an atheist city to avenge. At the head of this faction emerged the toad-like figure of Adolphe Thiers in *pince-nez,* long a favourite target for caricature by Daumier. This was a consummate political opportunist, who blew with any wind that arose, and had somehow amassed a huge fortune holding a number of government appointments. He leaned, if anything, slightly to republicanism so long as it fostered the interests of the *haute bourgeoisie.*

M. Verdier beamed the next time he saw Louise Michel. He had been among a group of unknown men, just citizens, who called a public meeting to discuss their reaction to proposed national elections, and proposals coming from the Government safe in Bordeaux to disarm the National Guard and to cut its pay. Michel had been invited but was too busy with her children's needs to attend.

"Five thousand people came!" Said Verdier,

"All the usual uproar! But they wanted to act! A motly crowd of Jacobin fossils, radicals, journalists and crack-pot artists, but floating on the tide of '48, the people: the makers and the doers with dirt on their hands and steady heads. We held them to it. We've convoked delegates from the National Guard to the Central Committee of the National Guard that we recently assembled. The National Guard represents all the manhood of Paris. They will not yield their arms to Bismarck or Thiers. The bastards hooted down Garibaldi at the Assembly in Bordeaux. He resigned the Paris seat. Now we have laid down the keel of a state here. We have charged a commission to move it forward. They stepped up and were appointed by consensus. All unknown. The middle-class, the small shopkeepers, the employees, the trades-men. Men of abilities more than ideas. Many strangers to politics. We let them assemble, we withdrew. The idea of federation is universal, not sectarian. Today Clement-Thomas resigned. He can no longer control the Guard. He called them to put down their comrades and they stayed in bed! We are issuing a proclamation that any threats, from Bordeaux or Berlin, will be met with arms. This here is the view of the clubs. He passed her a wall-poster. It read:

A declaration of principles. We seek by all possible means the suppression of the privileges of the bourgeoisie, its downfall as a directing class and the political advent of workers. In a word; social equality.

"At last!

"Let them hold their election of the few!" Said the printer. The French electoral system at the time would guarantee a bourgeois government.

"Have a meal with me, Louise. You look half-starved," He fetched a good vintage of red wine from the back room and they walked down to *Le Marmite* together.

Chapter Eight

Drunken Boat

Arthur Rimbaud sat in the café on *Place Ducale* in Charleville reading a newspaper. His bowler hat was in a puddle of beer on the table. The newspaper soaked a little of the beer up each time he laid it down, still open, and sighed in a way that turned the heads of French and Prussians customers alike. He agitated everyone. It was as if he might boil over at any moment. The barman was sure that when he arrived the café emptied a little. It set his nerves on edge. He came over to Arthur's table with a cloth to wipe up the beer.

"You'll spoil your hat, Arthur," he said feebly.

Rimbaud reached around the damp newspaper and put the dripping hat on his head. Some beer ran down his face. The barman wanted to pound him with his fists. He wiped the table, skirting around a little pile of Caporal Dark Shag tobacco. He desired urgently to sweep the tobacco aside. It took all the satisfaction from the job to leave it lying there.

"You should ask your mother for a nice tobacco pouch Arthur," he went on.

Rimbaud suddenly dropped the paper on the floor, screeched his chair back, thrust his legs out and released an explosive sigh that made the barman's heart knock in his chest.

"The Mouth of Darkness wouldn't give me the bogey off her fingertip," he said, raising a forefinger and wagging from side to side.

He grabbed the newspaper from the floor. By now it was un-foldable. He crumpled it into a shape that showed the article he was reading. Five minutes earlier the Charleville Examiner had lain crisp and dry on the bar. He jabbed a finger at it and held it under the barman's chin.

"Good job the bloody Krauts have defeated us," he said. And then, into the apprehensive silence,

"Us high-and-mighty Gallic heroes will never be able to strut our arses along the boulevards again! We're fucked! Mind you, it means the Krauts are stuck licking Bismarck's arse for good. Dictatorship for ever! Old spike-head will piss all over them now! Crowned Emperor in Versailles for fuck sake!"

This even-handed presentation of insults seemed for a moment to balance and neutralize the palpable sense of alarm in the room. The Prussians and the French looked at each other. They appeared to be seeking some kind of a lead as to what to do. A Prussian private soldier who was leaning on the bar turned to look at Rimbaud.

"Bravo Monsieur," he said quietly.

Half a dozen people of both nationalities walked out. Arthur threw the paper aside. He filled and lit his pipe.

"Why should I fucking well care," he said, to no one in particular.

Ernest Delahaye arrived, bought two beers at the bar and joined Arthur, who, in making room for his friend, jogged the glasses. Beer began to run in a little stream onto the floor. He leaned sideways and loudly sucked it into his mouth,

"Why waste good beer, eh Ernest? The price they charge for it in here. Daylight bloody robbery." Delahaye went back to the bar, picked up the bar cloth and wiped the table dry just before the liquid reached Rimbaud's pile of shag.

"They will be opening the school on the fifteenth," he said.

The news was too much for Arthur Rimbaud. He stood up. He walked up and down with his mouth open. He sat down again.

"How are they going to do that? The place is full of blood, brains and chopped-off fucking legs; fucking cripples tottering around on crutches moaning their fucking balls off; fat-arsed nurses blubbing and dribbling through their drawers in ecstasies of fucking compassion."

Only the day before Rimbaud held forth for ten minutes on the nobility of the science of medicine and with what pride, he, Arthur Rimbaud was a student at an institution that had become a hospital. "The poetry of healing" and "the art of life itself" had been among the phrases Delahaye remembered.

"They're going to use the town theatre for the time being," he said.

Rimbaud seemed not to have heard. He put his head on his arms and was silent for a good while. Delahaye filled his pipe from the slightly damp pile of shag on the table, lit up, and then doubled the size of the pile from the tobacco pouch in his pocket. He took a pull at his beer.

"Well I'm not going back to school," said Arthur in a muffled voice.

"I'm finished with it." He sounded sleepy. His shoulders rose in a deep sigh. Then he sprang upright with his palms flat on the table and leaned over Delahaye as if he were to blame.

"I'm going back to fucking Paris!" he shouted.

The barman felt a sudden surge of delight.

"And if the Mouth of Darkness chucks me out I'll go and live in the quarry."

He pulled up the sleeve of his coat and held his wrist-watch under Delahaye's nose.

"I'll sell me watch. That'll pay the fare."

"I thought you were planning to find a job," offered Delahaye, unwisely.

"A job?" shouted Arthur, "A jobby jobby? A big-job? *'Have you done your big-job this morning, Arthur?'* Yes Mama, I pooped it out into the fucking boggie boggie!"

Here he did straining-on-the-toilet movements with his hands on his knees. He got up and looked down at his chair seat.

"'Look Mama, it's swimming around with all the other jobbies. It's cuddling up to your huge big-job, Mama.'"

The barman was squirming. A customer picked up his plate and took it to the far side of the bar, where he tried picking at his food again.

"I could do a big-job here, Ernest. Right here in the café. Waiting tables. A big brown table-jobbie. You'll see. Everyone wants me to do a big-job for them. They give me prizes at school for my poetical big-jobs. Extruded from deep within my soul! Long, lachrymose, lyric jobbies. And lumpy, hard jobbies in alternating hendecasyllables, *squeezed out* Ernest, forced forth with agony through the rosy portal of my soul!"

The barman had had enough:

"You'll have to go if you keep carrying on like that, Arthur," he said.

"You see, Ernest?" Rimbaud was beginning to cheer up.

"We are fallen among Philistines."

To the barman:

"The long slow solace of an alexandrine jobbie!"

Delahaye glanced towards the bar.

"Drink up Arthur, let's go to the quarry," he said.

Just beyond Charleville there was a small wilderness overgrown with pine trees. Man-made limestone cliffs enclosed it on three sides. The cliff overhung at the back and was covered in ivy with limbs as thick as a man's arm. The ivy partly obscured an area which was dry and level under the cliff face. Delahaye and Rimbaud started coming there after their presence in the shed in the Bois d'Amour was discovered. They found two old armchairs thrown out along the road and carried them into the quarry. When they were pushed together they made a comfortable sheltered bed.

"If we can find some old canvass sheeting to cover them it'll make a perfect hovel," said Arthur.

He pulled the chairs apart again and they sat down.

"I'll succeed in making all human hope disappear from my mind here, Ernest. Silent as the predator I'll pounce on every joy and strangle it!"

Delahaye stretched his legs and lit his pipe. One of Arthur's poetic monologues was at hand.

"I arm myself against justice! Oh witches, poverty, hatred, it is to you my treasure is entrusted! I will summon the executioners so I can bite their rifle-buts as I die!"

He paused,

"Pass the fucking baccy Ernest."

He held the tobacco pouch aloft and waved it at the fuddled sky:

"Misfortune is my god. I will summoned up plagues and drown myself in blood and sand. I'll stretch out in the mud. I'll dry off in air heavy with crime. I'll play fine tricks on madness, Ernest, fine tricks. The whole town will come to poke the hermit in his lair. *'See children, this is what will happen to you if you forget your catechism!'* They will pick their way through my garden of turds!"

He filled his pipe and threw his leg across the arm of his chair.

"I am damned! I abhor my country. The best thing to do is to fall into a really drunken sleep. Oh Science! Everything has been appropriated. Be a scientist! Study. Learn. For the body, the soul. – the viaticum – we have medicine and philosophy – old wives' remedies – princes' entertainments – forgotten games! Geography, cosmography, mechanics, chemistry....Science! The new nobility! Progress! The world strides on.....or does it fucking spin? Eh, Ernest? *Ich spinne. Du spinnst. Ja! Wir sprechen eine mögliche cuntishsprache!* Puss-filled craters of pox! *'Give me an ounce of civet, good apothecary to sweeten my imagination.'"*

He paused to fill his pipe, puffed up a cloud of smoke, and was racked with coughing. He gasped and wept.

"Hungrily I await God. I have belonged to an inferior race since time itself began."

He gained in strength:

"Pagan blood returns! The Spirit is nearby! Why does Christ not help me by giving my soul nobility and freedom? My day is done. I am leaving Europe. Sea air will burn into my lungs. The furthest climates will tan my skin. To swim, trample the grass, hunt. Most of all smoke! Drink alcohol strong as molten metal! I will return with limbs of iron. Dark skin, furious eyes. From my mask it will be thought I belong to a mighty race! I'll have gold. I'll be idle and brutal. Women nurse furious invalids like these when they return from hot countries."

Ernest Delahaye reached into the ivy behind him and drew out two bottles of beer.

"Ernest, you're a fucking genius, that's what you are!" said Arthur Rimbaud.

The Mouth of Darkness relented on her demand that Rimbaud should return to school. It was not often she was bested, but the poor woman had recently seen both her sons disappear without trace into an all-out war. She hated Charleville in her way as much as her son. She would like to have conquered it through his ambition to rise. But the news of his behaviour got from reports brought to her by her daughter, Isabelle, gave her a curious pleasure. When Arthur spent nights in the quarry it brought the matter to a head.

"I will not permit you to return to that school, Arthur," she told him when he came back.

"Live in a freezing quarry by all means; but if you live in my house you'd better get yourself a job."

"I'll look in the khazi," said Arthur.

He wrote a letter to the Charleville Examiner. He was invited to attend an interview. The velvet suit he had been given in Brussels was brushed up lovingly by his mother. She helped him into it and patted his lapels. She crept up behind him and soaked his head with pomade. Furious, he went straight to his room and washed his hair in the basin. When he returned she had hidden his coat and boots. He found he had grown out of his school shoes. The four inches of hair that had grown since he was in Mazas prison in September stood out in all directions. And so it was that an enraged limping youth with an immobile expression and glacial eyes confronted a fat burger.

"I see here you believe you have what it takes to make a journalist," said the editor of the paper, glancing up and down the letter without looking at the boy or acknowledging his entrance.

"Why are you pretending you're reading my letter for the first time?" asked Rimbaud quietly. "You personally signed the reply you sent to me and alluded to its content, so you must have read it then."

"I can't be expected to remember every job application I receive!" The editor was amazed. He looked for the first time at the youth before him. There was a strong smell of pomade in the room.

"You're a journalist. That's exactly what you should be expected to remember," said Arthur Rimbaud.

An unpleasant silence set in while Arthur stared him down. The man coloured up.

"How dare you come into my office with that attitude?"

"I don't find it particularly daring," said Rimbaud. "You haven't pointed a gun at me yet. Look, do you want a journalist or am I just wasting my time?

"You are wasting your time in this establishment! Mister, Mister, what was it......Rimbaud!" He shouted, beside himself.

"With an editor who can't remember the name of the person to whom he is talking that's self-evident," said Arthur sweetly.

After school opened again Rimbaud spent most of his days in the quarry reading. He had stolen from the bookshop an eighteenth century French translation of

Jacob Boehme; Darwin's *Voyage of the Beagle*; and some periodicals featuring a serial called *Twenty-Thousand Leagues under the Sea: An Underwater Voyage around the World* by Jules Verne. At lunch time he met up with school-friends and cadged beers. He spent nights in the quarry. He had discovered tarpaulin on a haystack. . When it was tied up into the ivy it contained a space like a room. He had an oil lamp from the farm at Roche. There was room to light a small fire. Nevertheless the cold made him think of clothes. He had his father's farm-boots resoled. He wore two pairs of trousers as a tramp had taught him and the previous autumn. ("And tuck 'em in yer fookin' socks.") He wore six layers, ending in a waist-coat, a jacket and a greatcoat. The great-coat reached the boots.

His mother seemed to be glad to have him out of the house so long as she knew where he was. She even gave him some money. She fed him when he got home. Not a word passed her lips. Rimbaud learned that he could sleep quite comfortably in freezing weather if he curled up in the great-coat fully and wrapped his head in a scarf. It was not much warmer in his bedroom. In his hovel at night he read Twenty Thousand Leagues and dreamed poems of iron -- modern, air-tight, riveted; he imagined the crystal barques of the future, unknown mineral structures, subterranean worlds. He pioneered sciences of liberty and autonomy. Like the poet he would descend into his worlds, observant, curious, exulting, and fashion vessels of departure. When he blew out the candle, he closed the ports. The vacuum mechanism vibrated. Slowly the immaculate barque descended into the violet depths.

****

"Paris swarms with innocent monsters," thought Arthur Rimbaud, as he walked from his train under the vast filigree iron and glass sky of the Gard de l'Est. The square in front of the station was filled with carts, hand-carts, black cabs, bourgeois families, Mamma, Papa and a teenage-blond-girl in a blue bonnet; soldier, priest, a couple of urchins.

The urchins zoned in on Arthur straight away. In a world of blue-black military great-coats his old brown farmer's coat, the colour of Caporal Dark Shag, stood out. It set off the chocolate tone of the little bowler, thought Dip as he fell in step beside Rimbaud.

"Welcome to the City of Light *citoyen,*" he said.

On Rimbaud's other side a small girl put her hand in his.

"Do you have a couple of sous for a hungry man, comrade?" said Dip.

Arthur, quite naturally, disengaged his hand from the girl's and searched his pockets. He found five sous.

"All I got. Want them?"

Dip stooped down and picked up Arthur's pipe and tobacco.

"Look, you've dropped these," he said. The girl hugged Arthur's arm. Dip said,

"You have less money than me. Keep it. What's your line of business, citoyen?"

"I'm a poet," said Rimbaud.

"*Are* you," said Dip. He was taken aback, and pleased. "Do you know Victor Hugo? I know a poet. Mlle Louise Michel"

"Read him. Don't know him. Or Michel. I want to meet Verlaine."

Dip said,

"Look, comrade, if you need a place to sleep and some food ……." He gave Rimbaud directions to Pigalle.

"Ask for Mme Lemel at *Le Marmite.* She might be able to help you out. Got a place to go?"

"I'm looking for M.André Gil in Rue Git la Coeur."

Dip looked at the girl and they both laughed.

"What's so funny about that?" Rimbaud felt slighted.

The girl squeezed his arm again,

"We know him. He works for M.Verdier. He does pictures," she said.

Gill was a member of the Central Committee.

"Look mate, we'll walk you down there," said Dip. He turned to the girl,

"We can see what pickings there are south of the river, and get back in time to meet in the *Place de la Bastille.*"

"I think you're very nice," said the girl to Rimbaud, and took his hand again.

It was the first time anyone had ever said that to him.

Arthur felt suddenly free to be himself. As they walked he talked poetry. The girl skipped along, alternately grabbing his hand and hugging his arm.

"I will write poetry that will change life itself!" He realized with a start that Dip believed him.

"The poets have only interpreted the world, in various ways. The point, however, is to change it," said Dip, adapting a quote from Marx that M. Verdier had dinned into him. "It's the task of a revolutionary to struggle to change the world with everything he does! I was among the *canaille* that invaded the Legislative Council and made the fucking Toffs declare a republic."

"It was fun! It was fun!" shouted the girl, skipping about.

Arthur felt slighted again.

"I was in Mazas prison at the time," he said.

"What for?"

"No ticket. No fucking money."

Dip stopped and looked Rimbaud up and down.

"Just tell 'em you're fourteen. Can't bang you up then."

"I am sixteen years old," said Arthur severely, looking up at the urchin. He was to grow six inches by the end of the year.

"Oh well. Suit yourself. Just telling you." Said Dip.

They walked on in silence, along the desolate boulevard with its houses boarded up and the long rows of tree stumps lining the pavements.

"Tell us a poem then," he said at last.

They were just behind Notre Dame. The girl pointed at the cathedral.

"Bang! Bang!" she cried, and started giggling.

Arthur took a notebook from his pocket. Beside the long row of flying buttresses he read them *Bateau Ivre,* slowly, in an enchanter's voice:

> *"Sweeter than sour apple-flesh to children*
>
> *Green water slid inside my pine-clad hull*
>
> *And washed me clean of vomit and cheap wine*
>
> *Sweeping away rudder-post and grapnel."*

"That's fucking *good!*" said Dip when he finished. "Better than Hugo! Arthur, you're the fucking ace in the pack, man! That's what you are!"

"I know," said Arthur Rimbaud, passing Dip his pipe.

Outside the numberless house on Rue Git la Coeur the urchins and Arthur parted company. Four flights up he knocked on Gill's door. No one answered. He opened the door and walked into a mansard studio filled with illustrations and paintings. He looked at them all, taking big slugs from a bottle he found on the table. He finished off the loaf and the cheese. Then he lay down on the couch and fell asleep, shortly after discovering the absinthe.

Chapter Nine

A Season in Hell

While Arthur Rimbaud lay asleep Jules Favre was signing the terms of the capitulation with Bismarck in Versailles. The gunpowder smell of revolution hung between them. For all the fires and flunkeys, the vast palace remained cold. In Paris huge crowds, battalions of National Guards and units of the regular army had been assembling in *Place de la Bastille* day after day in defiance of the capitulation. When Dip and the little girl arrived there, twenty thousand people surrounded the July Column, the people's column that marked the revolution of 1830, which had deposed King Charles and revived the Republic. Big festive fires blazed here and there. It was cold, but the days were drawing out. In the gardens and parks the blackbirds had been venturing their first quiet sub-songs. They had started giving that nervy dusk alarm-call that sounds like a coin striking a bottle as the light left the sky. Dip and the girl wriggled through the crowd, diving between legs and under elbows, keeping up a bright, cheeky patter the while. At the Column Dip passed her a handful of banknotes which she put in her drawers. They watched as a worker, a steeplejack, started to climb the great brass, winged figure of the *Génie de la Liberté* which was poised on one foot with a torch held aloft atop a golden ball. Forty seven meters up he swung up onto its back-thrust leg, onto its buttocks and finally, hauling himself between its wings, shinned up the arm and mounted the un-furled flag on the torch.

When the red flag flew and the cheers went up, André Gill turned for home. The son of a count, he was a handsome, good-hearted man, dressed in the bohemian artistic style, with a thick mass of black hair and a waxed moustache. He sauntered along tapping the pavements of the dying city with his cane; but he felt anything but jaunty. He could see the country was on the edge of civil war. That morning the *canaille* had broken down the door of the Archbishop's palace. The angry mob confronted a greasy-haired, rheumy old man, the very image of a filthy priest, in his library. He told them that all he owned were his books, which, he thought, were of no use to the poor. A woman carrying a sword strode up and told him that they were quite able to read, but "not a lot of lies about God, and girls having babies without fucking someone first." The old man seemed to her to be senile. She called the mob off, and they left him alone.

In his studio on Rue Git la Coeur Gill lit a candle. He nearly sat down on Arthur Rimbaud, who was deep asleep. The bottle of absinthe was on the floor beside the couch. He picked it up and replaced it on the mantle shelf. Could the sleeper be a burglar? He held the candle up to get a better look at the angelic boy.

"What the fuck are you doing here?" He said quietly before giving the boy's shoulder a couple of gentle shoves.

Rimbaud opened his eyes, appeared to see nothing, closed them again, and turned over to face the back of the couch.

"Hey! Hey! You there! Wake up!" Said Gill in an affable voice. "What are you doing in my studio?" He shoved Arthur's back gently with the toe of his boot to reinforce the question, and when the boy groaned and stirred, he picked up the absinthe, sat at his table, poured himself a drink and awaited developments.

"Would you like another glass of my absinthe?" he asked the child, who had rolled over to look at him after stretching languidly.

"Alright. Why not? As you like," said Arthur Rimbaud, sitting up suddenly, and assuming a proprietorial attitude on the couch, leaning back with his hands behind his head.

Gill got a second glass, poured a good shot out, handed it to the boy and clinked his glass.

"Who are you?" He asked.

Arthur appeared to think there might have been someone else sitting beside him,

"Who me?"

He pointed to his chest.

"Me?"

He tousled up his hair.

"Rimbaud," he said, sank half the absinthe, grimaced and belched. Then, slowly, and with thespian gravitas:

"I am Arthur Rimbaud, the poet."

"And what brings you to my poor studio, M. Rimbaud?" Asked Gill, regretting the cliché immediately under the expressionless gaze of the boy.

"I've seen your stuff. I have come from Charleville to meet artists and poets. I got your address. Do you know Paul Verlaine?"

Gill dodged the last question. He was cold and tired. Perhaps the boy was a little mad, he thought.

"Take my advice and go back home to Charleville," he said. "There is going to be a war. The Prussians will be in the city at any moment. Get out of it. This is not a good time to be alone in Paris."

He passed Arthur a ten franc note.

"Go to Mme Rachou at No.9. She will give you a bed for a franc a night. Go home M.Rimbaud." He pulled Arthur to his feet, took the empty glass out of his hand, and with his arm round the boy's shoulders, patting him paternally, showed him the door.

"No. 9," he said.

Arthur returned downstairs. He walked out onto the street. He walked past No. 9 without noticing it. He walked down to the river. He was not looking for a place to spend the night. He was not looking for money. He was looking for poets. He wanted letters of introduction, addresses, the names of the café's where Verlaine drank; the bookshops where Hugo or Banville spent their afternoons. Had he gone to *Le Marmite,* as Dip suggested, he would have met Louise Michel and been introduced to Hugo sooner or later. She would have marvelled at *Bateau Ivre.* She also knew the address of the family in Montmartre of the silly girl whose head was being turned by Paul Verlaine. But Rimbaud had forgotten all about Dip. He was looking for the gateway to hell. He had some burrowing on his own account to do. Down there, Les *Fleurs du Mal* were grown explosive, their pistils dusted with gunpowder. Down there they might touch his face like the icy fingers of the blind; the great lilies of the catacombs sweating with nitro-glycerine. Down there he would find a suitable posy to present to the poets of Parnassus. He kept walking through the monstrous city. He walked all night.

The following day, 40,000 National Guards and units of the regular army, without their officers, paraded under the Arc de Triomphe in a show of force directed at the Prussians. Vinoy sent a force of Mobiles against the crowds in Bastille and it fraternized with the people. In Montmartre the two great drums started to beat. The Central Committee of the National Guard, that association of *Les Invisibles,* after a tumultuous meeting, asked the assembly to vote for removing the cannon that were about to be surrendered to Bismarck, from the boulevards to the working-class districts. L'Oursin and Franck drove a team of horses, got from mutinous Breton Mobiles, and hauled the guns from under the noses of the bourgeoisie units. They drove them past the Moulin de la Galette, bleak in the hard light of early spring. The horses slithered on the steep, rutted track. The women of Montmartre who had not gone to the parade, old women and children and a few old men, assembled under the windmill where the track was steepest, and helped shoulder the wheels and shove the heavy guns up to the Buttes.

In M. Verdier's shop, Dip was running the rotary press. He and the other lost children missed all the fun on the *Avenue de la Grande Armée.* They were fanning out across Paris with posters for the other teams. The Central Committee of the Twenty Arrondissements and the International were alarmed at the way events were running out of control. The city was on the edge of an uprising at the very worst moment. The poster laid out the dangers. It was not the time to take on Bismarck. Let him come and go. Let the blame for capitulation rest with the reaction. M. Verdier, who was a member of all three organizations, left Dip in charge and ran fast to the meeting of the new Committee of *Les Invisibles* in the Third Arrondissement. He and a few others prevailed by force of good sense over the Central Committee of the National Guard. To everyone's amazement, particularly that of a few conservative journalists present, they simply called for a show of hands and the National Guard delegates voted to avoid any confrontation with the Prussians. They then laid plans to barricade Paris off from the boulevards and to greet the occupiers with silence. The barricades demarcated the class divisions in the city. Last they put all hands to removing the artillery pieces from the parade to the Heights.

Arthur Rimbaud, meanwhile, was walking through what seemed to him to be a dead city. He lay down in a doorway in the St-Merri quarter where rue de la Verrerie met rue St-Martin. He slept comfortably for an hour or two. His tramp's clothing was quite adequate to keep out the cold. When he awoke a black cat was sitting beside him purring. He sat up and lit his pipe. The cat walked away around the corner. Arthur had discovered invisibility. To the invisible the world is all theirs. He made himself comfortable against the door.

Monstrous city. Night without End.

Later, just at first light, he skirted the deep mud on the road past the Moulin de la Galette and walked up into the smallholdings. The city below looked like a litter of bones, he thought. A blackbird was singing very quietly. He napped again under a fence and then descended towards the river and the booksellers.

The alchemy of the word! Mineral substrates ripe with mould. Books liver-spotted like the hides of old gaffers. Pustulant books. Toiling and troubling books. (Arthur felt the pages, caressed them between his fingers). A ton of books to descend through on the quest for dragon's blood, green lion, messages from other worlds. Scripts like whips. The Quran. Scripts like elephantine Sanskrit. Words like nature, like minerals and elements, formulae to change life itself. Books like continents to be exploited for resources to forge Modernity. Arthur Rimbaud had, perhaps, one unique insight. Words, stories, ideas were connected to the world, and not by force of agency. They were an independent part of it, like chemical elements, these ideas and forms shaped by man. They were instable and mercurial. If you could develop the techniques, they would provide formulae for festivals of disorder.

At mid-day Arthur quit the bookshops. He wandered into the lanes of the old Left Bank and found a run-down café. A couple of Federal Guards and an old man were drinking red wine. He ordered absinthe. He drank until his head was reeling and then lurched off into the street. He bought a loaf and stuffed it into his pocket, tearing bits off as he walked. The city of Baudelaire seemed to have withdrawn into itself like the horns of a snail. Baudelaire was the human form of a snail, slowly caressing the city's breasts with his cold mouth, thought Arthur Rimbaud, who was touching it with his own feelers and recoiling.

The following day the Prussians entered Paris with a small cavalry detachment escorting a gun-crew with a team of horses hauling one of the great long-range siege pieces that had been battering Paris. It was a symbolic first step before the formal entry and parade to be held in a couple of days. Perhaps Bismarck was testing the water. A few carriages followed behind along the *Avenue de la Grande Armée*. The entourage stopped at the *Arc de Triomphe*. The ladies got down on the arms of their officers, some French officers among them. A photograph was taken. Suddenly a figure in a short, extravagantly ruched and flared black dress with a mass of centre-parted ringlets of unruly black hair framing the white face of a dell-Arte gamine came running from one side and turned three cartwheels through the group of ladies and their beaus. Monelle was gone before the officer's hands reached the hilts of their sabres, leaving the shriek of a wild bird on the air behind her. As if on a signal the great drums of Montmartre began to beat. There were no Parisians in sight. The company laughed and looked gallant, but the ladies soon got back into their carriages.

Monelle had been taking one of the lost children to newly discovered relatives south of the river. The Federation of the National Guard had begun to act as an informal police force by communicating enquiries about missing people at their central meetings. The boy found his aunts and was reunited with his sister. She brought the news of the Prussian unit at the *Arc de Triomphe* to M. Verdier, and then to Nathalie Lemel. Then she went up to the circus field to help the perfumer move back into her house. Spring was coming fast, and the old lady and the circus master were feeling the need for a little more space.

"When you've fought at a barricade together you can always share a bed," said the old woman, out of the blue. Monelle did not pursue the matter.

L'Oursin was back in his hut in the circus field. He brought some wood down to the house behind the Moulin de la Galette on the back of the mule and helped light the stoves in Monelle's room and in the perfumery where the old woman slept.

Two days later the Prussians held a parade that marched under the *Arc de Triomphe.* It was sullenly ignored by the people of Paris. Only the street kids came, and scored a few direct hits with half-bricks, until a child from south of the river was shot dead by a French officer. The Prussians stayed one symbolic night and then left. It was all over. Only the drums of Montmartre kept beating. When the last of the Prussian bands passed out of earshot the deep drums were pounding as they had throughout the parade, and throughout the night of the occupation.

March began, and with it the election that returned conservatives and monarchists across France. Adolphe Thiers was at their head. The Government crept back into Versailles, into the palace just vacated by Bismarck. Until the war, and its occupation by the Prussians, the Palace of Versailles had been more or less empty, of no consequence to post-revolutionary France. Louis Napoleon had lived in the Tuileries in Paris. Now it became the grandiose theatre of the triumphant Bourgeoisie. Perhaps they no longer needed an Emperor to embody their self-regard. The rich poured out of Paris and quintupled the population of Versailles. A great celebratory mass was held on the fields of Satory, recently the site of the Prussian encampment, heralding a week of celebrations and balls. The Government, under the chandeliers of Louis XIV, began to administer the new dispensation.

Arthur Rimbaud was aware of none of this. He had soon run out of money and was sleeping on the pavements in out-of-the-way corners near the bookshops. He spent the days reading occult and satanic literature, particularly the works of Elias Levi, in a favoured bookshop whilst picking pieces off a kipper he kept in his pocket. The bookseller was beside himself with rage. The shop stank of kippers, there was kipper grease on some of his most valuable volumes. The horrible boy dodged under his arm if he tried to bar the door to him in the mornings. He ignored him completely or gave him a nasty stare when he asked him to leave. Paris was in a state of lawlessness. His renowned clientele had gone to ground, and now, out of the nightmarish vacancy, had come this terrible bowler-hatted youth who seemed to exhale a miasma of violence and who knew more about literature than he did. The boy was the moment made manifest so far as the bookseller could see. He was the future. Without him the shop would be empty. He started to think seriously about moving it all to Versailles.

After about a week of this the bookseller felt a change in the atmosphere in the shop. He hazarded to peep around the shelves at Arthur's corner. The table the youth occupied was vacant of books save for a pamphlet. Rimbaud had read pretty well all of the French literature of occultism and Satanism while he had been there. He looked beatific and calm. The bookseller was charmed. The youth had piled up two columns of small coin on the table.

"Oh hello," he said.

He picked up one of the columns of coins.

"Will you take this for the pamphlet? That'll leave me enough for another kipper, you see. Wonderful library you have here."

Rimbaud got up and put the money in the bookseller's hand.

"See you next time I'm in Paris," he said.

The bookseller nearly wept.

Out on the street Rimbaud read the first newspaper he had bothered to look into since he arrived. The events it described seemed bland and unreal after the occult underworlds he had dived into. It was daylight, calm, ordered and pleasant. He bought a kipper and a small loaf with the last of his money and sauntered off to have a look at Paris.

In *Le Marmite* there was uproar. A crowd of angry people filled the street outside: National Guards with their Chassepots with fixed bayonets; the ubiquitous sword-bearing *Mariannes* of working-class Paris; the old veterans of '48 wearing tattered red sashes; whooping street urchins and excited dogs. The Versailles men of order and civilization, the priest-craft, the squires, the Bourbon rump, the unbuttoned paunch of the *Haute Bourgeoisie*, the bankers and investors, the Government of Adolphe Thiers, egged on by a shorn Jules Favre and the Blimps, had passed a series of edicts. All the progressive newspapers were to be closed. The Vigilance Committees and the Clubs were to be closed. The National Guard was to be shorn of the 1.50 Fr pay that kept half of the poor in Paris from starvation. It was to be disarmed. The pawn shops, that during the siege were forbidden to sell the items they held, were to be allowed to trade them for cash: the seamstress's scissors and work-benches; the carpenter's tools. All back rents on the miserable apartments of the poor were to be paid within a month. All debts had to be settled, this edict causing hundreds of thousands of small businesses across Paris into default overnight. Bismarck's indemnity was to be paid in full by the poor and the small trades-people of Paris. At the same time he sent the regular army units and the rural mobiles home, leaving Vinoy with a few thousand mutinous troops. Such rural regiments that remained had been fed by the poor of Paris, who brought provisions to their bivouacs in the Bois de Boulogne. Soon, exhausted and radicalized by privation and defeat, most were deserting and moving into the population. Thiers, who only knew how to extract rents and play one side off against the other, had made the Commune inevitable.

M. Verdier's shop was producing a dozen different posters that replaced the banned newspapers. The teams of lost children got them up across Paris. Flourens and Blanqui, who had both been sentenced to death in absentia, wrote their own rebuttals that were up in every street in Paris within hours of publication. The Central Committee, which Thiers called a secret society, but which had always published its minutes in the radical press, responded by putting the names of all its members on a red poster which invited Thiers to attend a meeting. One, authored by Victor Hugo, repeated the plea he had made to the assembly in Verailles on behalf of the poor. He had been hooted out of the assembly. The posters told how the government-appointed commander of the National Guard had sent an envoy to the Central Committee demanding surrender of the cannon. The Committee threw him out. A second envoy "went over to the people." Cartoons of Thiers came from André Gill. Manifestos, proposals, lunacies and rants shouted from every corner. Emaciated, gaunt Paris was a city of tongues, of mouths crying; of clamorous typography.

The word clamoured at Arthur Rimbaud as he wandered the shorn streets along boulevards lined with tree-stumps, sand-bagged public buildings, boarded up houses strident with posters. He walked under the barbaric skies of early spring, Paris everywhere, rising up. He passed women of the *canaille* whose hands bent backbones (he thought) hands that ladled poison out, dark hands. He crossed the Seine at Neuilly Bridge and walked twenty kilometres up the long, straight road to Versailles. He was chased out of the palace gardens at nightfall. The town was filled with noble ladies and the young dandies of the boulevards. It was brilliant with light and money. He was invisible, a creature outside the light, a demonic, bowler-hatted shadow that made one or two people start back. He wandered back towards Paris through the night, sleeping occasionally for a couple of hours by the road. It was his second day without food.

Dawn in Paris: a city without a bourgeoisie. The misty Bois was empty save for some peasant-like woodchoppers. In Batignolles he wandered the streets of tenements as people were getting up and emptying their piss-pots into the drains. The smell of shit, coffee and freshly-baked bread made him wild with hunger. He climbed through the cemetery of Montmartre. Shortly he saw a large, shabby café which had a poster on the door that read "Penniless? Hungry? Then Eat!" The poster was illustrated with a cartoon of a skeletal man tucking into a plate of food that Rimbaud recognized was by André Gill. He had found *Le Marmite,* although he had no idea of it. He walked in. A robust woman was sitting by the door drinking her first cup of coffee and smoking a cigar.

"I'm hungry," said Arthur pathetically.

Nathalie Lemel looked him up and down.

"Of course you are," she said. And,

"Sit there."

Arthur sat.

"Battle-heavy breasts," he thought.

Lemel went into the kitchen and put pans of cooked food on the range to heat. She prepared a big plate and put a loaf beside it in front of the boy.

"You can take the rest of the loaf away with you," she said.

She sat down and watched the kid eat.

"Petty bourgeois. On the run. Flighty. Thinks he's tough. Something odd. He'll do fine," was her judgement of Arthur Rimbaud.

After a while, when he had smoked a pipe and finished his coffee, Rimbaud got up to leave. He shuffled towards the door.

"Take your fucking plate back into the kitchen and wash it up," said Nathalie Lemel mildly.

Arthur did as he was told, but not very well, as Lemel predicted. She didn't wish him goodbye.

He found his way east, through Belleville, where an immense flow of people was beginning to assemble and move towards Bastille. It was difficult not to be caught up in the flow, but his feet took him away from it. Rimbaud was always a tangent to all spheres. Eventually he came upon a walled necropolis and wandered into it to find solitude. He had found Pere Lachaise. He lay among the tombs without a thought in his head listening to the apocalyptic conversations of the birds, enjoying the unequalled sensations of youth and a full belly. After a while he got up to look at the bust on a plinth above his head. He was lying on the grave of Balzac. He lay back down again and stretched like a cat. He rolled on his side, fished out his pipe, and lit up. Then he ambled through the funereal shade of a stunted forest of the dead that made the mausoleums and tombs appear to be constructed already beneath the earth. In the darkest heart of the place he found the tomb of Molière. Rimbaud was astonished. He stood below the bones of the master, or so it seemed: the tomb comprised the great block of the sarcophagus raised on four squat, square stone columns adorned with bronze wreaths. It was as if the entire tomb were already rising up towards paradise, as if the earth were too corrupt to touch the remains of the poet. Arthur lay down under the cataphalque on the dull, white limestone slab and presently fell into a long dreamless sleep.

When he awoke the city appeared deserted again. Notre Dame stood up before him; a Medusa of blackening priest-craft after the trenchant simplicity of Molière's tomb. He recoiled from it and followed the river against the flow until he came to the Canal Saint Martin. He followed it north. As it began to get dark the tow path and the canal entered into a tunnel. Every fifty meters there was a feeble gas light. Canal barges were moored along the path, a few with dim lights aboard. Slowly, alerted by his unfamiliar footfall, the barge dogs started barking. It was the greeting of Cerberus he thought. Shouts went up to silence them. He was walking beneath Bastille, under the foundations of the July Column. After some while, in a long silent space, he saw a barge filled with coal under tarpaulin sheeting. He carefully pulled the sheeting up, slipped beneath it and pushed the coal about until he felt comfortable.

He came awke again to the sound of water lapping against the barge. He could see it was light outside. He carefully peeped out from under the sheeting to see open country. A furious dog leapt at him and pinned him down under the cavass, snarling and walking on his body.

Someone called the dog off, the canvass was ripped back and a man collared him and dragged him out. A cuff round the head made him see stars.

"Jesus, Mary and the fucking Pope but there's no peace anywhere these days! "

"I was sleeping," said Arthur reproachfully, rubbing his ear. The dog looked at him and began to grin and wag its tail.

"And now me fucking dog likes yer," said the bargeman.

"Was it you as fuckin' found 'im then?" (To the dog).

"I'm going to Charleville," said Arthur, with as much dignity as he could muster.

"I see. Well you're going the wrong fucking way, Mister." He whistled the horse which was up along the tow path on a long rope. The horse stopped dead. The bargeman grazed the barge along the bank to bring it to a stop. He pointed across the fields.

"Find a fucking road and go that way. Charleville is about fifty kilometres over there. I've took yer half way fer nowt. Now you can fuck off."

Two days later Rimbaud was back in Charleville. He ran into Delahaye coming out of school in the town theatre. Delahaye was shocked at his appearance.

"You look like you've been down a coal mine, Arthur. Are you alright?"

"Never better, Ernest. But I ran out of baccy and I need a beer."

They headed for the café on Place Ducal.

Chapter Ten

Les Invisibles

Louise Michel spoke from the pulpit in the church that housed the Vigilance Committee of Montmartre. The building was packed. Children ran riot through the side chapels releasing flights of echoes that circled the roof like bats. A dull roar sustained the sound, and over it all the clear and distinct voice of Michel, making a joyful and contemptuous poem of resistance.

"The Bishops are riding those Bourbon donkeys of the Shires into Jerusalem! The Holy City of Versailles! Versailles! That gilded piss-pot stinking with the foul vapours of the Elohim of Monarchism! Napoleon risen! Kyrie Napoleon! He shines over us in his little silver-buckled shoes slippery with the blood of the people! In his white, worsted stockings, spattered with our gore! Shall we nail him up? Shall we put a pistol bullet in his groin?"

Here she pulled out the revolver Monelle had used in Notre Dame. The crowd roared. She opened the gun and slowly put six rounds in it. She held it up.

"I have this to greet Emperor Louis with if he sets foot in Paris again! This is my negotiation with the forces of Reaction! This is my rosary of led for the Priests of God!

This blunt argument! Rise up the people! For we are banned! We are outlawed. We are silenced! That jackanapes Thiers has opened his greasy chaps and pronounced the closure of this Vigilance Committee! We are closed! We obey! Dagobart, King of the Franks, limps towards us with his broken sceptre! We tremble! Come, the fat little homunculus, Thiers! The mandrake, the forked root! We'll harvest him with this!"

She stood down. She was still holding the loaded revolver. She went out into the street holding it and did a round of the revolutionary clubs with it in her hand. She was working twenty hours a day, but with the slight increase of food in the city she had begun to eat more and looked fit. The high forehead, the generous mouth, the short jaw, gave her face unusual power. She thought of herself as ugly with a kind of pride. It set her free. She thought of herself as impulsive, wild, unpredictable, often foolish, often irrational, a zone of instability, even madness. She refused to rein it in. She was her own revolutionary chaos. She had begun to live the way she would live the rest of her life, in a state of permanent murderous and suicidal insurrection. She made no bones about it. She was at war with Power and desired no mercy. If they had any sense they would kill her now, she thought.

Georges Clemenceau tried to negotiate a settlement between Thiers and the Central Committee of the National Guard in Montmartre over the disposal of the cannon. The Committee of *Les Invisibles,* actually M. Verdier, whom Clemenceau knew well, told him firmly that they stood between Thiers and a return to monarchism. There would be no backing down. Paris was pretty well united on the issue. It had become a city without a *Haute Bourgeoisie,* without a ruling class, without the social stratum of dominance. It was evident in the strange atmosphere of vacuity that Rimbaud had felt. And it made no difference to anything. It was simply a space. The preposterous class of accumulated wealth and power had vanished like a bad smell. It was evident they served no purpose to society at all.

In Versailles, under the chandeliers, in the exquisite restaurants, at the balls, often forced to camp out in cramped rooms because of the influx of six times the original population, the fashionable and the *galant* sparkled with an effervescence of angst and bile. They saw in Paris a dark population, the insensate ground upon which they had always built their lives, the base-layer of the eternal, fecund poor that by its very nature was made to hold them aloft, beginning to grow discernible, to individualize, to clamour, to produce a seismic shift, to atomize and crumble. It never crossed their minds that they themselves were not necessary to society. Perhaps they were incapable of making that cognitive step. Among them were human and decent people who had wept over *Les Miserables.* But they genuinely felt that it was they who represented humanity, they who were the face of it, the intelligence of it, the class that wrote the great novels about it, the class that bestowed reform always, which made judgements. It was self-evident that ability was always and only discernible through money. Their position at the crown of the social hierarchy seemed to prove it. They were decent, moral people, of course. And they *were* the world. They represented society, they patronised its culture, were its scientists and foreign adventurers. Now they wanted their capital and rents to recover from the siege. They were the reason 150,000 small incomes were forced into default. They needed their money working again. But the siege had stopped the dispossessed from generating surplus wealth. Now the very small businesses that owed them money, that owed them rent, had banded together to hand over Paris to democracy, to the *canaille.*

In Paris the shopkeepers unpaved the streets around the cannons nearby thus making them more difficult to move. The National Guard watched over them at night. Thiers blustered, there were approaches, Vinoy kept up appearances in the *Hotel de Ville* with a few mutinous troops. They believed their own blandishments. It was impossible to imagine that the *canaille,* the shabby common rabble of Paris, the drunken, consumptive citizen soldiers, the grocers, the stone masons, the washerwomen, the cooks and whores could face down the French State, the men of order, property and the Church.

Louise Michel kept her own watch on the cannon of Montmartre. The school, where she lived with her mother, was at the foot of the Butte on the Pigalle side, a few streets from *Le Marmite.* She climbed the Butte first thing every morning. She communicated between the Vigilance Committee and the men. She became a kind of informal officer. There was a universal acceptance of her authority.

For her part she gravitated towards the terrorist spirits she found there, men as defiant and in love with death as she was. They gave her a kepi to put on her head and were enthusiastic when she organized a supply of rifle cartridges for target practice from her friend Émile Eudes, whose military background had led him to command of a regiment of National Guard under the Government of National defence during the siege despite his Blanquist leanings. The men instructed her in the use of the heavy Chassepot rifle. They taught her the basics of fighting with a bayonet and a sword. She was as good as they got, they said fiercely, whenever there was mockery of their dealings with a woman. They invited all comers to cross bayonets with her and gain some wisdom. She brought her old friend Victorine, Eudes' wife and her blood sister, up to the Butte. Victorine began to rival Louise in the speed and accuracy of her shooting.

Half way through March, Thiers and the Blimps twice attempted to remove cannon from Montmartre with a small force, in the belief the National Guard there would back down. They were repulsed by the *canaille* as well as the Guard. Thiers had been warned by the men of property that there would be no return to business until he crushed the rabble in Paris. Vinoy and the Blimps conferred. In the small hours of the 18th of March they brought in a force of 40,000 mixed and disaffected troops and gendarmes against the people of Paris to restore order.

Monelle was awoken just before dawn by a commotion in the street outside the Moulin de la Galette. Before she got to the door a shot was fired. Outside troops of the regular army had overrun the guard on the cannon beside the windmill. A National Guardsman was down, wounded, and three other local men had been overwhelmed. The old perfumer arrived and cleared a space before her with the piss-pot. She threw it at the head of the officer in charge, making him duck and draw his sword. Guns were levelled at her. She stood her ground, hands on her hips and denounced them with a voice like a grinding knife. Suddenly this old crone had dominated the scene. All eyes were on her until a soldier hit her between the shoulder-blades with the butt of his Chassepot and knocked her on her face. Monelle got between her and the soldier and covered the old woman with her body, but she was getting up already.

"Get the Master and L'Oursin. I'm fine. Then go to Nathalie. Get the kids out. M.Verdier and Louise too. Get people awake!"

Monelle ran. By now a large force had ascended the Butte from the north and were in possession of 170 cannon on the terraces. Or so it seemed. The National Guard there were talking to them. A bottle of wine appeared from the derelict house. As she ran down from Heights Monelle cried the streets awake. Women were getting out to the bakeries. She roused Lemel and Verdier and woke up the House of Lost Children. Dip selected a team and told the others to keep in doors. Returning up rue Rossier she shouted to the gathering crowds of women to defend the cannon. A group of women and children had already started to move uphill. The crowd swelled, local Guards joined it; last the men.

Headed by a hundred women and urchins it ran into a detachment of troops bringing three cannon down from the windmill. The women had plunged between the ranks before the soldiers knew it. They grabbed the heads of the horses and drew them up in spite of the yells from the team drivers. The general in charge, General Lecomte, rode up in the rear with sabre drawn and ordered the troops to fire on the rabble. A sergeant shouted a countermand. The troops raised the butts of their rifles as a sign they would do the people no harm. Lacomte in the background waved his sword in the air and shouted orders to fire. By now food and wine had arrived. Women of the Clubs were exhorting the troops to defend the people. An attempt was made to rescue the wounded Guardsman from near Lacompte. He and his officers refused to let anyone near.

Louise Michel, alerted by Monelle, went straight up into Montmartre towards the *Mairie* and the church where the Vigilance Committee met. She ran into Georges Clemenceau, furious at the presence of troops on the streets. Thiers had informed none of the mayors. Clemenceau sent her to the Buttes to see what was going on. She went up on the north side and found the troops beginning to limber up the guns, rather unwillingly, yelled at by their officers. She walked blatantly into the derelict house, where some troops and National Guard were drinking. L'Oursin and Franck were there. She picked up a Chassepot and a handful of cartridges, looking straight at the regular soldiers, detached the long sword-bayonet and concealed the rifle under her greatcoat. She came running down the hill crying "treason!" At about this moment a party of National Guard cut Lecomte off from the rear. The officers surrendered and Lacomte was dragged from his horse. The crowd surged forward towards the Buttes where it met Michel, now with the rifle in her hands. She turned back. A white light enveloped the Heights like a sign of deliverance. The birds were singing. She was certain they were all going to die. But the officers above had other problems. A mob of Clubs' women, among them Dip's gang from Pigalle had overrun the descending cannon. They cut the traces and let the horses run free. The gun detachments raised the butts of their rifles in surrender. On the Heights the troops raised the butts of their rifles. In any case there were no more horses. Vinoy had forgotten the need for horses to move cannon. The officers sheathed their swords and went along with it. L'Oursin, with a loaded Chasspot in his hands regretted it wasn't a saxophone.

Georges Clemenceau, who half an hour earlier had been pleading with General Lacomte to allow him to take the wounded guardsman to a hospital, and had received the answer "I won't let you display this martyr across Paris," now found himself rescuing Lacomte from the mob and giving him shelter in the *Mairie.* Shortly afterwards Lacomte had a companion. General Clement-Thomas, the butcher of '48, had been recognized in broadcloth and topper come as a spy to see for himself what was going on. A couple of Clubs' women carrying swords had recognized him and collared him. They shortly threw him in through the doors of the Mairie, dishevelled, red-faced and hatless. All over Paris there was a full-scale revolutionary insurrection underway led by furious working-class women and children.

In Place Pigalle a mob of drunken prostitutes dragged an officer from his horse, killed him with his own sword and then used it to butcher the horse and distribute the meat to the neighbourhood. *Le Marmite* took possession of a haunch from a woman bloodied up to her chin.

It was 10.00 a.m. before the Central Committee of the National Guard, *Les Invisibles,* was convened in the church of the Vigilance Committee of Montmartre to the sound of the Montmartre drums beating and half the churches of Paris ringing calls to arms. They found themselves called upon to facilitate a revolution they had not expected. The army of the reaction had surrendered to the people. Louise Michel was there, Théophile Ferré, Raoul Rigault and other Blanquists, who were well represented in the Committee of *Les Invisibles.* The more sober men of the Committee shut them up in short order. M Verdier, in the chair, cross questioned Émile Eudes for military advice. They had little need of it. Vinoy had made desperate calls for the bourgeois National Guard, hitherto loyal to the Government, to come to their aid. When only a few hundred turned up Thiers panicked. He fell back with the last straggle of his troops to the *Champs du Mars* where he declared the evacuation of Paris and fled to Versailles, emptying, at the same time, Mount Valerian and the outer forts to provide him with a rear guard. Able men of the National Guard across Paris took the surrender of the remaining battalions and of the Gendarmerie without the need for instructions. The posters of Thiers, still wet, announcing a "return to order" were enough to prompt them to act. By mid-afternoon the *Hôtel de Ville* had been occupied. A frantic jockeying for power by bourgeois "leaders," who saw power as their right, ensued. They went to the Central Committee for endorsement, imagining it were in charge. The Committee were civil servants, not power brokers. They were civil society, not a proposal for government. They refused to endorse anyone, and it was only with the greatest reluctance that they agreed to meet that night in the *Hôtel de Ville*.

Up at the Montmartre *Mairie* the *canaille* was in uproar. They had heard that the butcher of '48 was there. The old perfumer was at the head of a mob that notwithstanding the pleas from Clemenceau charged doors. The two generals were dragged out of the building and stood up against a wall in Rossier Street. It was a scene later illustrated by Andre Gill, who was in the crowd. The old perfumer, with a sword in her hand directed the execution. Lacompte, repeatedly begging for mercy, had no impact on her. Louise Michel, leaning on her Chassepot, thought that General Clement-Thomas died well enough.

In the house behind the Moulin de la Galette the old perfumer propped her sword behind the stove. Monelle found it hard to look her in the eye. She could kill a man in anger, but execution was beyond her understanding.

"It'll be time to start grinding orris soon," said the old woman brightly.

L'Oursin and the circus master arrived. The circus master took the old woman in his arms and rocked her from side to side.

"Don't you start, you senile old git," she said. "I've got enough on with this one," (indicating Monelle), "get the fucking animals back here, and let's start living our lives again."

The freed gun-carriage horses had been captured and brought to the circus field. The tent was in Montmartre, with the generator and the props. They were more or less equipped to make a circus as it stood. The Master wrote to the farm in the Meuse valley, where his Algerian illusionist had gone. He proposed the return of the ring ponies and the dogs when he thought it was safe to do so. L'Oursin and Monelle sought out the other circus acts that had dispersed across Paris during the siege; some into the army, never to return. The tent went up in the field on the Heights. The masts flew red oriflammes, the forked pennants flown by the Gallic kings in battle that signalled no surrender, no quarter.

In the *Hotel de Ville* the revolutionaries took the floor. They called for Paris to march on Versailles. The force in Paris could have overwhelmed the National Government there with ease. The majority of the Committee refused it out of hand. They stood on principle. They were people used to building barricades, not assuming dictatorial power. They had no mandate until municipal elections could be held. Their demand was only for democracy and a measure of self-rule for Paris. But they turned away the liberal and conservative mayors who like Clemenceau clamoured for a surrender of the cannon and a return to order. They also secured key institutions, the Bank of France and the

Ministries of Finance and the Interior; the Naval and War offices. They placed a Committee member, Émile-Victor Duval, the son of a seamstress, in the *Prefecture de Police.*

In Versailles Thiers cried up class war in a secret session. They would defend "order and society." There would be no concessions to the *canaille.* They ruled out any reply to a message received from the Central Committee that called for their support in conducting proper municipal elections in Paris. They were aware that this was the sum of the Central Committee's aims. Thiers made it quite clear that they should give the rabble of Paris its head while they prepared a force out of rural France with an excuse for bloody repression. The monarchists and churchmen in Versailles are recorded in the minutes of this meeting specifically calling for "class war" waged by the bourgeoisie against the workers of Paris. They were unequivocal about it. They planned for a massacre on the 22end of March.

For their part the *canaille* cried for autonomy and social justice. They wanted socialism. They wanted an end to sixteen hour days and cold and hungry children at the end of them. That is what *La Commune* meant to them. It meant dignity. The bourgeoisie hazarded a counter-demonstration of top hats that fled the boulevards under gun fire. In the *Place du Hôtel de Ville* 20,000 National Guard camped out with bread on their bayonets cheering the Master, L'Oursin and Monelle's *Commedia dell'Arte* antics lampooning Thiers and the men of order. A rank of cannon was drawn up in front of the building. The sun came out. The crowds came out before the *Hôtel de Ville* and along the boulevards where they addressed one another as "citizen" and did the bourgeoisie who had remained in Paris and who dared to venture out into the balmy day no more harm than to address them as equals. They assembled on the Buttes of Montmartre among the cannon. The Moulin de la Galette reopened with a scratch-band hastily put together by L'Oursin and Monelle. The Montmartre seamstresses came out in their borrowed finery and they danced for the first time in six months.

Victor Hugo returned to Brussels. Louise Michel brought the news to M. Verdier late at night after his meeting in the *Hôtel de Ville.*

"Hugo's no revolutionary," said M. Verdier.

Michel kept a tight-lipped silence. Then she said,

"Victorine and I have been conscripted by Eudes. He's preparing for war!" M. Verdier held her gaze. He said,

"We have received 700,000 Fr from the Bank of France and a sizeable loan from Rothschild. Now we can pay the Federal Guard." He meant the newly-named National Guard. The name-change was one of a series of symbolic actions the Commune was to make.

Hugo, in Brussels, knew what no one yet knew in Paris. The Bank of France, which *Les Invisibles* were too principled to seize without a democratic mandate, had given, at the same time, three hundred million francs to Versailles to build an army against the city.

The Central Committee of the Twenty Arrondissements wanted nothing, could aspire to nothing, but to serve the will of the people. It had not made the revolution. It did not see itself as a revolutionary force. It dismissed the approaches of the Mayors who went so far, Clemenceau blustering at their head, to demand the return of the *Hôtel de Ville*. The entire building, save for the Committee room at the front of, was filled with plebeian Paris, arguing and debating. The Committee indicated the joyful crowd in the square and the battalions of Federals camped there.

"Make your demands of them," it told the unelected Mayors. "We are holding an election in two days. After that, whatever the outcome, we will stand down."

The election returned revolutionary and Jacobin republican candidates across Paris. The Blanquist Raoul Rigault, on the run since the shoot-out of the 21st of January, stood in the wealthiest quarter of the city comprising the new boulevards around the *Arc de Triomphe*. It was true that most of the householders were in Versailles, but their servants, who outnumbered them ten to one, voted for social revolution. Paris was pretty well unanimous in its support for an autonomous, republican authority. It also supported its predominantly socialist character.

The Commune was inaugurated with a display of symbolism that was to characterise its brief life. The Federals descended on Paris from Montmartre and Bellville, a sea of bayonets topped with red pennants. Many were wearing the Phrygian cap, the Liberty Cap of 1793.

The great drums of Montmartre beat incessantly while making their slow progress towards the *Place du Hôtel de Ville.* A steady and measured cannon-fire sounded from the Heights. The *Hôtel de Ville* was hung with red flags. Inside, the Central Committee was grouped on the public platform with the new members of the Commune wearing red sashes. Their names were announced. Some speeches were made punctuated by cannon salutes. The Committee declared its mandate at an end, stood down and disappeared into the crowd although eleven of their members had been elected to the Commune and remained on the platform. Louise Michel, in the crowd, exultant, later recalled: "It was a spectacular opening for the Commune whose grand finale was to be death."

Dip and the Lost Children put panniers on the mule and went around the streets of Montmartre and Pigalle begging for coal to fire the circus generator. M. Verdier printed some tickets to hand out to the generous. The circus seamstresses freshened up the costumes with a dry-cleaning preparation, basically petrol, pioneered for cleaning clothes in Paris only a few years previously. Every clothes-maker in Montmartre had a can of dry-cleaning spirit in her house. The circus animals arrived, looking their best, following the Algerian Illusionist, dressed in his eastern fantasy costume through the streets in perfect order; five dogs and three horses with not a tether or a lead between them. They had come from near Charleville on a canal barge, paid for with one of the circus-master's gold Louis, sewn into the Algerian's green silk turban. He was an atheist who knew most of the Koran by heart and used it, with scatological interpolations in modern Arabic, in all his magic spells. He was a member of the International Workingmen's Association.

Before March was out the generator fired up, the brilliant white electric lights went on in the ring and on top of the four masts. The lights on the big tent became the principle sight of Paris at night. The Master put on two shows a day, most people coming in free or for a small donation, and he still made money. M. Adolphe Sax, so long in conflict with Paris over the rights to his invention, came every night and was feted by the crowd when L'Oursin demonstrated the latest member of his saxophone family, the great contrabass saxophone. Sax lifted his topper and walked the ring, bowing to the audience, which raised a fantastic ovation of bravos as Monelle, in pink and blue, danced the dogs, and L'Oursin played. It was the first time Sax had felt a welcome in Paris. When Nathalie Lemel insisted he took on apprentices, whom she would feed, he was pleased to do so. His workshop, provided with cut-price materials through the *Le Marmite* network, began producing instruments again. The Commune approved purchases for the bands of the Federal's regiments.

Late March was mild, bright, windy and uplifting. The dispossessed crowded the boulevards. They poured into the reopened Louvre. The Tuileries Palace, six months previously the home of the Emperor, was opened to the public. The *canaille* explored the bed-chamber of the Empress. They were reminded that the treasures were now the possession of the people and quite effectively policed themselves. The rag-pickers and washerwomen of the slums composed themselves on Eugenie's fine sheets and down pillows for a moment and closed their eyes in bliss. Many had been forced to pawn their bedding during the siege.

The pawn-shops were reined in again and forced to return essential items on demand, in exchange for agreements to pay the principle and not the interest. Landlords were forbidden to evict tenants in arears. The pawn-shop owner, the concierge and the priest, the principle enemies of working class Paris, just recently so fierce and arrogant, were now made compliant and timorous. The removal of their grips on the throats of the poor was the single most palpable effect of the revolution. And it was felt as strongly in Versailles. The bourgeoisie had been cut off from their plunder. The class of rentiers had now no income from their investments in misery. Their bankers threw up their hands when approached for liquidity. What could they do? Until the rabble in Paris was ruthlessly crushed the representatives of civilization and order would have to borrow at rates of interest that reflected the risk. The rabble! The riff-raff! The mob! The *canaille!* The vile multitude! These were the mythic and terrible undertow of society. Civilization rose through them, it floated upon them like some vast, bright ship. The common people were the stormy sea that supported this ship of state; both indispensable and perilous. They floated it; and the bourgeoisie knew it in their bones.

M. Verdier's roller-press started printing newspapers. The banned progressive papers had been set free to publish. No moves were made against the reactionary press, however, which was virulent against the Commune, depicting it as a vile riot of murderers, rapists and child killers, drunken and gore spattered. Thiers encouraged these calumnies and distributed the papers among the assembling armies of conservative Rurals on the plain of Satory near Versailles. He also quadrupled their wine ration and added a good tot of rum to it. A foreign observer, hostile to the Commune, described them as resembling a Tartar hoard. Thiers appointed the most conservative and monarchist generals he could find to drill them into shape. When some battalions arrived chanting for *La Commune* their ring-leaders were promptly shot and the rest shipped out to Algeria.

Chapter Eleven

Storming Heaven

When Victor Hugo left Paris it changed Louise Michel. She was not in love with him. She was in love with Théophile Ferré, a Blanquist romantic twenty years her junior, a slightly ridiculous little man with a high, strident voice in whom the fire of revolution and fearlessness burned as powerfully as in her. She thought of Hugo as her poetic master. If he had left Paris it was his own affair and it did nothing to diminish him in her opinion. But it powerfully reinforced her sense that life itself was poetry: beyond the page, the poetry of the real, lived, inspired, ecstatic. It was a poetry she shared with Ferré, and its muse was death. And like all poetry it was inextinguishable. As Hugo had written: "No army can defeat an idea whose time has come." Michel understood that it was possible to embody an idea. It went beyond the world. Perhaps it was a kind of immortality.

The Commune, surrounded on every side, by the Prussians, as by the Versailles reaction, had only death on its horizon. In the *Hôtel de Ville,* Jacobin and Revolutionary alike proposed a meticulous adherence to principle and law. They prepared to defend Paris until the forces of monarchism and property came to their senses. They were reasonable, decent men, and like all reasonable, decent men found it difficult to understand arrogance and savagery. They were men who worked and made, without reliance on accumulated capital, property and rents. Thus they were inherently free men, and thought as free men think. They had no real sense of Power and the State. They had, rather, an instinct for free interaction, horizontal dealings, for the devolution of interests, business-like, trusting, co-operative, not hierarchical, not accumulative. Power, for them, like the work they produced, was intended to be distributed outwards, to be used. Their surfaces in contact with the world were osmotic, inter-penetrative. The skin of the Bourgeoisie, on the other hand, was like the skin of a bladder. Thiers even came to resemble a paunch with a face.

Michel, because she was a woman, did not have a vote. Radical France, the heirs of Proudhon and Blanqui, was immovably misogynistic. The International Workingmen's Association, despite its name, was alone in welcoming women and proposing universal suffrage. Nevertheless she was at the heart of the revolution through her membership of the Montmartre Vigilance Committee and her friendship with two of the major actors in the Central Committee, Raoul Rigault and Théophiile Ferré. The men had both been nominated by the Commune to run the police. Rigault had a history of insurrection against the Empire and owed his life to the painter, and habitué of the Moulin de la Galette, Auguste Renoir. The previous summer he had been hiding-out from the very police he now commanded in the forest of Vincennes near Paris, starving and in rags. Renoir, out painting in the smock and beret of his trade, had come upon him among the trees. He left his easel, returned to the village, and brought back painter's clothes in which to disguise the fugitive whom he accompanied back to Paris and sheltered in his apartment. Renoir's seamstress partner and model of that time later fought behind the barricades. This was after she walked out on him, angry at his refusal to engage politically, but that is another story. During the spring of the Commune Renoir was arrested as a spy by Communard Federals while painting by the Seine. They threatened to shoot him on the spot. He quietly told them he was a friend of Raoul Rigault who immediately released him over a brandy in the boulevard café in Paris where Rigault conducted business. Renoir was to painting, perhaps, what Louise Michel was to revolution. He was quite fearless and painted outside the security of the Paris walls throughout the Commune.

Louise Michel sat at a café terrace with Rigault and Ferré one early morning in late March drinking coffee.

"If the Commune will not attack Versailles as we should have done on the 19th of March, I shall go and shoot Thiers personally," she said.

"For God's sake Louise, how on earth could you get to Versailles on your own! In any case you would be recognized immediately" Ferré's , voice rose and broke on a falsetto.

"Quite easily. Come with me, if you are not afraid."

Rigault was furious.

"Neither Theophilé nor I are afraid of anything!"

She laughed in their faces.

"Then let's go," she said.

"For Christ's sake, Louise!"

Rigault made the mistake of attempting to browbeat her,

"The shooting of Lacomte and Clement-Thomas has done the Commune enormous damage across France. The murder of Thiers would only strengthen the hand of Versailles. We need support from the provinces, not condemnation. If I thought there was the slightest chance you could get anywhere near Versailles I would arrest you now!"

"Very well!" Michel stood up. "I am persuaded by your reasoning."

She looked down at Ferré, who coloured up.

"But this is the last time either of you will underestimate a woman!"

She went straight up into Montmartre and knocked on the door of a seamstress whose children she taught. Within an hour the woman had fitted her out in a turquoise, bustled, silk dress with a pink parasol and matching bonnet. Her husband was a cab driver. The family were members of the Montmartre Vigilance Committee. By mid-morning Michel was being driven to Versailles. She had frequently been depicted in the conservative press, and had an instantly recognizable face, but the bonnet had a veil to it and no one at the checkpoints thought to question a bourgeois woman. The rich were still moving freely from Paris to Versailles. After a brief tour of the town she went to the military camp at Satory, got down and addressed a company of Mobiles enjoying the spring sunshine. She praised the Commune and exhorted them to follow her back to Paris and defend the people. The soldiers raised a cheer. An officer stepped forward and took her by the arm. She thought he had arrested her, and so did the men, who started to stand up, until the officer signalled his good intent. He said to her,

"I want to join the Commune. Can I get into Paris?"

She took him back to the cab. In the back she lifted her veil.

"I'm Louise Michel. Let's find some paper and a pen and I'll write you a letter of introduction to the Chief of Police, Raoul Rigault."

In a café in town she wrote,

"Citizen Rigault, I present to you Citizen Jules Dupont, whom I met in Versailles. He would like to join General Eudes, but, in the interim, puts himself entirely at your disposal for any task useful to the cause. Here then is Citizen Jules Dupont, whom I recommend to you as a good citizen and our friend. Salutations and equality!" [13]

She visited a bookshop in his company and that of the cab-driver and amused them by telling the proprietor what a terrible woman Louise Michel was. She bought the

Versailles papers, said goodbye to Dupont and returned to Paris by sunset. By this time Rigault was quite drunk, as was usual with him. Neither he nor Ferré recognized the elegant woman who dropped the Versailles papers on their table until she lifted her veil.

"Expect Lieutenant Jules Dupont from the Breton Mobiles with a letter from me. I persuaded him to desert," she said, and climbed back into the cab.

There is little doubt that Michel could have killed Thiers had she chosen. The Assembly in Versailles was open to the public and she was an accurate shot with a revolver. Rigault was standing beside her when she pinned down the Breton Mobiles at the windows of the *Hôtel de Ville* on the 21st of January at a range of fifty meters, perhaps saving his life when the friend at his side was killed. He and Ferré looked at each other in horror as the cab rolled away. Michel was foolhardy, perhaps, but she succeeded in every endeavour she set herself. She threw herself into what she called "the poetry of the unexpected." It was a definition of revolution. She was to become a formidable warrior.

At the end of March Thiers sent a force against the Communard defences between Versailles and Paris. At first the Versailles officers had to drive their men at pistol-point to engage their fellow Frenchmen. It was an exploratory engagement and succeeded in capturing thirty Federals. Vinoy was unambiguous. All Communard prisoners were to be shot at the point of their capture. Any Versailles soldier not obeying this order would be shot too. Thirty men faced the firing-squad in the bland spring sunlight.

The murder of the prisoners of war demanded a response. Much has been made of the inefficiency of the Commune, of its inability to organize militarily. Setting aside the truth that decency and an instinct for freedom are poor qualifications for organized violence, the fact is that the Communards were outnumbered five to one by now. Had they pursued Thieres and Vinoy to Versailles and put the *Haute Bourgeoisie* to the sword in the first place they might have conformed to the standards for political excellence of later conservative historians. But revolutions, before they are betrayed, are invariably vitiated by brotherly instincts. They would not be revolutions otherwise. It is how we deal with the exercise of power that defines us. The bourgeoisie, the Church and the monarchists might have decided to respect a huge popular mandate for municipal autonomy in Paris and negotiated with it. They did not do so because they did not believe that the majority of their fellow citizens were fully human. We always dehumanize the people we enslave.

Eudes, Flourens and the men of action, who had proposed taking Versailles on the 19th, were now given their head. Louise Michel and Victorine Eudes, in the 61st Regiment of Federals from Montmartre commanded by Émile Eudes, waited to move off in the *Champs du Mars* at 3.00 a.m. under the stars of early April. Michel had paid her debts, handed the running of the school over to her assistant and lied convincingly to her mother about her role in the conflict. She was to be a nurse, safely behind the lines, she said. She carried in her pocket a series of letters to her mother, entirely fictional. She had acquired a new

Remington carbine, a more reliable and faster-loading weapon than the Chassepot. For the first time since she left the Tomb twenty years previously she was free. She had nothing to think of but the present, the incomparable realm of love and death.

Michel cut through the chaos of the Federal's advance and found her way to the furthest point of their push towards Versailles by first-light. Cannon-balls were ploughing up the embankments of the Versailles road, dominated by the heights above Clamart which had been retaken by the Versailles artillery the previous day. She delighted in the howl of the incoming fire and the violet smear of crushed flowers along the path the balls tore in the turf beside her. That night, after a day under heavy artillery bombardment in the trenches near Clamart village, she led an assault on the Versailles line on the hill above them, only five kilometres from the Palace, and well defended with machine-gun emplacements. Eugène Razoua, who commanded that section of the advance, a professional soldier with a reputation for impetuousness, did not realise that the soldier ahead of him was a woman until he threw her his sabre to rally the men and heard her voice cry out "to Versailles!" She walked upright upon the red flashes of the machine guns, caught up in the beauty of the scene, while methodically placing shots at the exact point of their fire until the fire ceased. She came close to taking the first Versailles' trench alone, but there was no one left alive anywhere near her, so she calmly went in search of Razoua, who persuaded her, with difficulty, to retreat on Clamart again.

The gunners on the heights above Clamart had found the range of the Federal trenches. Michel was surrounded by terrified men. She was afraid herself, but fear was not a negative emotion for her. She found it exhilarating, and thought hers was a woman's perspective. The exhilaration stemmed from her ability to detach. She told her companions that men were naturally more faint-hearted than women:

"A woman may feel ripped open to her very womb," she said, as the shells fell with the regularity of clockwork nearby, "but she remains unmoved. Without hate, without anger, without pity for herself or others, she can say 'It must be done.'"

She was succumbing to hyperbole. The truth was that she loved danger. She was later to write:

"Was it sheer bravery that caused me to be so enchanted with the sight of the battered Issy fort gleaming faintly in the night, or with the sight of our lines on night manoeuvers, filing past the slopes of Clamart, or heading for Hautes-Bruyères, with the red teeth of the mitrailleuse flashing on the horizon? It wasn't bravery; I just thought it a beautiful sight. My eyes and my heart responded, as did my ears to the sound of the cannon. Oh, I'm a savage alright, I love the smell of powder, grapeshot flying through the air, but above all I am devoted to the Revolution." [14]

Five years later, exiled on the Pacific island of New Caledonia, she was to precipitate an insurrection among the indigenous, cannibal tribes there that nearly drove the colonists into the sea.

A soldier nearby crawled along the trench to her side. He was an African Zouave, very black, in a red turban. His teeth were filed to points.

"In my country the men run when the women fight!" He announced to everyone.

He laughed for a long time. Eventually he shook Michel's hand. He turned to the others, pointing to his mouth,

"That's why we do this to our teeth! It protects us from our wives!"

He and Michel were to fight side by side for the rest of that engagement. He was well-read and thoughtful. He put his hand on her arm one night and said,

"We have a wide river to cross, Louise."

It was always necessary to fight off Versailles advances to prevent the bringing up of machine guns. Michel was mention in dispatches in the Communard newspaper *Journal Officiel:*

"There is an energetic woman fighting in the Sixty First. She has killed several men."

Georges Clemenceau saw her in action, and later wrote, a little curiously, because this is what warriors always do:

"In order not to be killed herself she killed others…..I have never seen her to be more calm. How she escaped being killed a hundred times over before my very eyes I'll never know, and I only watched her for an hour."

He might have borrowed a Chassepot and found out for himself. He was fifteen years her junior. But he had work to do in Paris.

More than once Michel rescued men she had wounded. The Commune had made it clear that wounded Versailles fighters were to get the same treatment as Communards. It also paid their widows, if they remained in Paris, the same pension as Federals. On the other hand the forces of Versailles routinely fired on ambulance nurses in the field and promptly shot them if they were captured.

One night a strange young man was directed to Louise Michel. He told her that he was opposed to the Commune, but that he had received permission to visit the forward trenches in order to develop a statistical theory. He was a student. He sought to test his equations in locations of particular danger. Michel invited him to drink coffee with her in a section of the trench-line that had been abandoned because it received repeated direct hits. A number of men had been killed there. They carried a table and two chairs with them. To her delight Michel discovered the student had a copy of Baudelaire with him. She read aloud from it while he made calculations in a notebook, noting down the times and locations of near hits. The men nearby were furious with her. Then the Zouave arrived, kicked the student out of it and dragged Michel away just before a cannonball smashed the Baudelaire to pulp and fragmented the table.

Michel picked herself up and looked round for the African, but he had disappeared. She didn't see him again for a couple of days.

The Communards were forced to retreat into Clamart village where Michel was put in charge of the guard on the munitions dump in the railway station. The Versailles forces had brought more artillery onto the heights, including guns firing explosive shells. Clamart was becoming a charnel house. Women arrived from Paris to work as ambulance nurses and under Michel's influence started carrying arms and firing back when fired upon. These were women out of uniform, the revolutionary dispossessed of the Clubs acting on their own initiatives. A husband of one of these women came looking for his wife and was directed to Michel who was in the most dangerous location in Clamart. He was in a state of complete terror. After Michel located his wife, who dismissed him, she took advantage of her friendship with Eudes to send the man with a letter to the commander:

"Dear Eudes: Can you please send this imbecile back to Paris? All he is good for is to create panic if there were people here capable of being panicked. I've convinced him that the cannon shots from our side are actually from Versailles so that he will run away quicker. Please send him away." [15]

She was less than candid. There was considerable and justifiable panic in Clamart. The village was being fired on from three sides now and was in danger of being cut off. It was beginning to look like a rout. Michel had earned a powerful influence on the men around her, but they were close to breaking point. They begged her to retreat. She told them to leave, lit a candle and sat before the powder store preparing to blow the place up when the Versailles forces arrived. The African appeared and sat down at her side. They delayed the retreat until transport arrived for the ordinance and then made an orderly move to the fort at Issy. There the Clubs' women rallied under a bullet-pierced red flag and organized the transfer of the wounded to Paris. The men were exhausted, weeping, or asleep where they lay. Michel and the African were alone that night, mounting guard while all the others slept.

"What impression do you have of the life we're leading?" Michel asked him.

"It's like reading a picture book," he said.

The Federals briefly retook part of Clamart, desperately trying to keep up with Michel, who was shaking her head as the bullets that whistled around her as if she were shaking off flies. She occupied the Clamart graveyard with a few men until forced to retreat again at first light. Before dawn there had been a night skirmish among the graves, lit up by the flashes and then only illuminated by the moon that made visible, white as ghosts, the gravestones behind which burst the rapid lighting of rifles. It was poetry of the unknown that entranced her while her methodical and accurate shooting gave time for her comrades to retreat. Then she and the Zouave got up and simply walked uphill together to the fort, under artillery and rifle fire all the way, talking like a couple on a country outing. Climbing back into the fort she slipped and nearly broke her ankle. It was the only injury she was to sustain.

The battle along that part of the line bogged down at Issy fort. Her blood-sister, Victorine Eudes arrived. Mme Eudes had distinguished herself further up the line. Eudes, who had heard about Michel's impetuousness, was surprised she obeyed his order to return to Paris. There she bathed, visited her mother, borrowed a one-horse buggy and drove straight to the thickest of the fighting at Neuilly Bridge where she put herself at the disposal of General Dombrowski, a Russian army officer turned revolutionary and perhaps the most experienced Communard commander. She never saw the African again, nor was able to discover his fate.

At Neuilly, prevented by her injury from making sorties against the enemy, she started to train the women arriving from Paris to be nurses. She received considerable hostility from some commanders: not Dombrowski, who like his compatriot Peter Kropotkin, was astonished at the misogyny of the French left. Nevertheless she found it necessary to write to Eugène Varlin, a founder member of *Le Marmite* and a minister of the Commune whom she knew well, for authorization to get food for the women volunteers, particularly a number of prostitutes there, who had retaliated against officers telling them that nurses should have "pure hands" with explicitly vulgar abuse that delighted the men who were more used to free women. There were class distinctions in the Commune too.

Michel stole weapons for the women and trained them in their use. She rode roughshod over any objections. Neuilly Bridge was under concentrated fire, including grapeshot, and opposition too her did not last for long. It became clear that her women, in mop-caps and petticoats, to save the few clothes they owned, were noticeably more audacious fighters than the men, perhaps because they were more motivated. These were the unruly women of Paris who had made the revolution. Most of them were to die later on the barricades.

When the nursing teams were established at Neuilly, Michel drove across Paris to Hautes Bruyéres, south of the city, to help train the women there. Here she met Jules Paintendre, a teenager who led a gang of street kids fighting alongside the men in the trenches. He was called the Commander of Lost Children, but knew nothing of the House of Lost Children in Pigalle His comrades were as reckless as she was, Michel thought; so great was their daring it did not seem they could ever be killed. On her way back to Neuilly she stopped at the printer's.

"Where's Dip?"

"He's around," said M. Verdier.

Michel told him about Paintendre.

"Keep them out of the fighting," she said.

"They're of more use to us here." He looked at her. His brother had been shot aged fourteen.

Back at Neuilly she found that Dombrowski had brought up artillery and a fierce fire-fight was underway. The shells were falling all around the church beside the bridge, the concussions setting the old medieval bells booming. The church had received some direct hits. She co-opted one of the unruly women to help her clear debris from the mechanism of the organ and operate the bellows.

"Let's storm heaven!" She shouted.

She played an hour-long, tumultuous improvisation around the sound of the gunfire and the bells. A Federal officer arrived and told her he had been ordered to shoot whoever was playing the organ. The sight of Louise Michel gave him pause for thought. He put away his revolver.

"You're attracting fire on the church!" He shouted over the thunderous dissonance of her playing.

"Good!" She shouted back joyfully, "It'll direct it away from the men!"

Chapter Twelve

Tortured Heart

Arthur Rimbaud stood near the bandstand in Charleville's Station Square and shouted "That's it! Order is overturned!" The three old burghers on the bench ignored him. Only the blackbird, carving the air with a song like liquid obsidian, paused and regarded the boy through its gold-ringed eye. Rimbaud noticed. When the bird started up again he shouted once more "Order is overturned," like a town crier. He did it more to shut the bird up than to enlighten the town. So far as Charleville was concerned it was in any case not true. The Prussians and their allies, the local business and land-owning French, were fully in charge. When Rimbaud got to the office of the pro-communard newspaper, *Les Progrès des Adennes,* where he had found a job, he discovered it had been closed by the authorities. He stood for a moment staring at the notice pinned to the door. He was late and had missed his colleagues. He tore the notice down and ripped it up, scattering the pieces all about him. He fished in the pocket of his coat for a piece of charcoal and wrote "Shit on the Church" on the wall beside the door. A couple of passers-by tutted and one laughed. Rimbaud told them to fuck off and went to the café to cadge a beer.

There he found his colleagues talking to Charles Bretagne, a Falstaffian figure, a petty tax official when he bothered to turn up for work, who relished the arts, and the occult, and who was well qualified to hold forth on Cabbala as well as details of the more outlandish sexual practices. He had taken Arthur under his wing when he returned from Paris, impressed by the boy's knowledge of Satanism. Bretagne was intelligent and ironic. He recognized the same traits in Rimbaud. He understood that the youth was a poet, first and foremost, and not an occultist. He had a powerful beneficial influence on Rimbaud. He was one of the few people who understood Arthur's intellectual achievements in his youth.

Bretagne was drunk. Beer glasses and a bottle of brandy crowded the table. He pulled a handful of connoisseur's shag out of his tobacco pouch and put it in Arthur's hand. He nudged the boy towards a long monologue on communism, the alchemy of the word and the fecundity of shit. He leaned back and delighted in it. He knew just how privileged he was. The company raved and soared. Alcohol blazed in their souls. Before he sank into seated oblivion he said,

"Go back to Paris, Arthur. There's nothing for you here."

A week later, penniless and footsore, Rimbaud walked into Communard Paris. The Federals at the entrance to the city passed him the bottle, gave him some tobacco and had a whip-round for some cash for him. As the bourgeoisie poured out of the city their numbers were being replaced by a stream of indigent youths, the flotsam of war, seeking the Promised Land. Rimbaud was one of many. It was late in April. The Versailles forces were ever more threatening, and gunfire from the west of the city punctuated the bird song everywhere. Arthur boasted of his service in the National Guard in Douai, and delivered a well-received, alcohol-inspired lecture on Communism. One of the Federals was going off-duty and decided to take him to the Babylon Barracks. The place was a sink for the insane, the psychotic, useless deserters from the Versailles forces and foreign adventurers on the make. He did not intend Arthur should stay there. He had a friend among the detachment of Communards attempting to keep order, and suggested they send the boy straight to the local Federal battalion for training, with a personal recommendation from him. Arthur had other ideas. The name "Babylon Barracks" entranced him. He would find the Parnassian poets the next day with new credentials as a revolutionary fighter-poet. The Federal shrugged and went home. He had just returned from Neuilly Bridge. Two of his children had died during the siege.

The warehouse Rimbaud entered stank of shit. The first thing he noticed was two people his own age, a black-haired girl in a flounced red dress and a red-headed boy in a bandsman's uniform sitting on the floor in a corner looking very alert. Everyone else was drunk. A group of men in the ragged uniforms of the regular army turned from the boy and the girl to watch Arthur entering the room. He stared straight back at them.

Weird-looking sturdy types. Many of them have exploited your worlds. Wanting for nothing and in no haste to bring into play their brilliant abilities and knowledge of how you think. What mature men! Eyes bewildered like summer night, red and black, three-coloured, steel pricked out with golden stars; deformed features, like lead, blanched, on fire; caprices of hoarseness! The cruel swagger of flashy rags – There are some young people.....[16]

Someone hit Rimbaud hard on the side of the head and he went over. He was on his hands and knees, dazed and crawling,

"Up we get my little darling."

The men passed him from hand to hand, laughing and jeering,

"You must learn not to look at your betters like that, my cherub!"

The men had seized upon Rimbaud after sizing up the girl and the boy. There was something un-nerving about them, the way they just sat there, relaxed but attentive, not reacting.

The soldiers forced Rimbaud face-down over a table and pulled his trousers down. There was uproar. One man parted his buttocks and spat a gob of tobacco juice between his cheeks. Monelle sprang forward with a knife in her hand and slashed the soldier opening the fob of his breeches across the face. Blood was running down her arm to the elbow. The man she had slashed was screaming, backing off with his hand to his cheek. L'Oursin grabbed Rimbaud with the hand not holding a knife,

"Pull your fucking pants up!"

Three Federals with rifles and fixed bayonets were suddenly there. They appraised the situation immediately, and stepped aside to let Monelle, L'Oursin and Rimbaud escape.

L'Oursin, in the street outside, tried to steady the boy, who was shaking.

Monelle wiped the bloody knife and her arm on her dress.

"You'd better come with us," she said, and gave him a quick hug. Arthur was crying.

It was cherry blossom time. The Japanese trees with their deep cerise flowers that had been planted along the river and near Notre Dame had mostly survived the siege. The wood was nearly impossible to burn. Monelle sang *Le Temps des Cerises* acapella, like a war-cry, in a harsh nasal voice as they walked along. It echoed with the blackbirds and the sound of distant gun-fire. It turned heads. This interpretation of the song as an anthem for a doomed revolution had originated with her and spread throughout Paris during the Bloody Week in May. The velvet blue of the sky, the shocking beauty of the blossoms, the carved voices of the blackbirds, the deep, stomach-wrenching sound of the guns and this voice, now, always now, under the brutal mass of the cathedral, silenced Rimbaud's strident inner clamour. He relaxed under the influence of a more powerful spirit than his for the only time in his life.

They took him to the House of Lost Children and made up a bed for him. Dip had enlisted in the Montmartre Federals and was with Franck in a gunnery unit at Issy. The girl who had been his assistant when Arthur met them in February was with a foster-family and was now a pupil in Michel's school. Nathalie Lemel recognized him and taught him to wash plates. The kids loved him. They showed him street games, hop-scotch, how to skip. This was Arthur Rimbaud's only childhood. He abandoned his pipe. The kids wouldn't tolerate it stinking up the place. He stopped drinking. He avoided adult company. Rimbaud always had the ability to change completely. He did it again, permanently, when he abandoned poetry and became a merchant. Now he became a child.

An official from the Commune informed the circus master that he was now to receive a grant from the Government of Paris. He made no demands on the Master: he should just carry on as before. Gustave Courbet, who had often visited the Montmartre circus, had arranged it. He had been elected mayor of the Sixth Arrondissement with responsibility for art in the Commune. It was Courbet who was to decree that the Vendôme Column, made from the bronze cannons captured at Austerlitz and crowned with a statue of Napoleon Bonaparte, was to be demolished. It was pulled down with cables attached to steam-winches cheered by a tumultuous crowd. Courbet secured the Louvre and sand-bagged its windows in an attempt to protect it from incendiary shells that he correctly predicted would be fired indiscriminately into Paris by the defenders of civilization. It was an explosive shell that burned the

Tuileries Palace to the ground, an event still attributed to the rabble, to women incendiaries, by historians of the victors. He secured the Bibliothèque Nationale, personally manhandling the Versailles-supporting librarian and physically kicking him into the street. The man had done nothing to protect the collection. Courbet moved the most precious books out of the city. He abolished the Academie des Beaux Arts, initiated a Union of painters and created a system of art education intended to free painting from bourgeois taste. This impulse was the foundation of the art of the Belle Époque.

Monelle and L'Oursin received a big hand-out from the Master. Monelle gave most of hers to the lost children and to the families of those children fostered across Montmartre. She had an elaborate, strange dress made for Louise Michel, black and decorated with black beads, pieces of obsidian and polished flint. Michel was in the front line near Versailles at the time. . Monelle laid the dress out on her bed at the school. We see Michel wearing it in photos taken after she returned from exile ten years later. The pawn-shops were now closed and their contents handed back to their owners. The seamstresses of Montmartre were flourishing. They danced wearing their creations at the Moulin de la Galette on Sundays during that glorious warm May.

Arthur was taken by the Lost Children to see the sights. They went to the Louvre, and crept about in awe and wonder. In the Tuileries Gardens they came upon a concert, an orchestra playing the *Symphonie Fantastique* of

Hector Berlioz under the astonishing beauty of the May sky and the cerise cherry blossoms. They sat on the grass among some of the few bourgeois families who had remained in Paris. These people were becoming more confident to go out in the atmosphere of general goodwill. People addressed one another as "citizen." The strange, opium-inspired music sounded to Rimbaud as if Charles Baudelaire haunted the gardens. He lay on his back with his eyes half closed surrounded, he thought, by Baudelaire's heavy-breasted whores who exhaled a scent of sweet corruption from their skirts as they swept by. The lost children became no longer instinctively predatory. They mixed with the children of the boulevards, admired their clothes, accepted some treats from picnic hampers. But it was they who felt they were the hosts. The crowd in the gardens was predominantly working class; the Palace was hung with red flags. This was suddenly their Paris. The Imperial Palace belonged to them. They felt generous. The fecund music seemed to be dreaming them all equally. Arthur Rimbaud fell asleep where he lay. He dreamed of elaborate eastern cities and the gardens of Babylon.

He woke up when the music stopped. The kids wanted to take him to the *Hôtel de Ville.* The streets were crowded and festive. Everyone seemed to be carrying a new revolutionary publication touted by kids in red caps. They watched the *Théatre de Guignol* puppets in a crowd of shrieking children, Rimbaud hissing and cheering with the rest. His transformation into a child was complete. They held his hands. They taught him songs which he learned attentively. They passed the massive barricades on the rue de Rivoli. At the *Hôtel de Ville* they walked straight into the building. It was crowded with citizens talking politics, arguing, making speeches. Rimbaud stood up on a table and elaborated the speech he had made on communism to the Federals when he entered Paris. He earned considerable applause. He was Liberty's child. *Marianne,* bare-breasted, leading the people with a red flag, seemed to attend him.

In the committee rooms laws were being passed, debates went on all day and far into the night. Historians of the wage-slavery we call Freedom, the intelligentsia in the service of business, the liberal-left consensus as well as the right, still ask what this revolution intend to "put in the place" of Capitalism, as if Capitalism had itself ever any intention, or planned for anything but the ascendancy of the few. Did Capitalism plan for Climate Change? Or is that its palpable legacy of greed and chaos? The Commune didn't plan. It did it. It did not fail. It was savagely repressed in the largest massacre until the Armenian genocide by those who later preened themselves on being the creators of the Belle Époque and the defenders of art, culture and civilization.

The Commune abolished conscription and the standing army, and declared the sole armed force to be the Federal Guard, in which all citizens capable of bearing arms were to enrol. It remitted all payments of rent for dwelling houses from October 1870 until April, the amounts already paid to be booked as future payments, and stopped all sales of articles held in the municipal loan office. Foreigners elected to the Commune were confirmed in office because "the flag of the Commune is the flag of the World Republic." At all levels all officials and functionaries were to be elected and all were to be removable by those who elected them. The highest salary to be paid to any employee of the Commune, and therefore to its members, was not to exceed 6000 francs, although no money was in fact ever paid to anyone. The Commune decreed the separation of the Church from the State, and the abolition of all state payments for religious purposes as well as the transformation of all Church property into national property and the exclusion from schools of all religious symbols, pictures, dogmas, prayers; in a word, "all that belongs to the sphere of the individual's conscience." Across Paris churches were appropriated by the people to be used as schools, workshops and social clubs. In reply to the shootings day after day of captured Commune fighters by the forces of Versailles, a decree was issued for the imprisonment of hostages, but it was never done. The guillotine used for public executions in Paris was publically burned at the foot of the statue of Voltaire in front of a massive, cheering crowd. Factories and workshops that had been abandoned by their bosses when they moved to Versailles were reopened as worker collectives. A workshop opened in the Louvre for weapons repair elected its foremen. The pawnshops were finally closed completely and the articles held in them returned to their owners. Credit facilities for workers were arranged. The Chapel of Atonement, built in expiation of the execution of Louis XIV was raised to the ground. Night-time baking was banned on the grounds that bakers had a right to sleep at the same time as other people. Women of fallen Federal soldiers were given pensions along with their children, legitimate or not, who also were to receive free education.

These acts, symbolic, or targeted at the needs and dreams of the dispossessed, were a celebration in themselves. They also had far-reaching political consequences. The dispossessed and the small owners had combined democratically to change their worlds. The impossible had happened. A class other than that of property, land and church was calmly reordering reality and the sky did not fall, chaos did not well up. The Bank of France, which contained enough money to buy Versailles, was left un-plundered. This was construed by the *Haute Bourgeoisie* to be weakness, not principle, of course. It was just one element in the fantastical outpouring of the unthinkable that was happening in Paris. The bourgeoisie who remained in Western Paris were not slaughtered. The defenders of civilization in Versailles found that fact itself to be somehow intolerable. They were free to return to their homes at any time by simply accepting the right of their fellow citizens to rule. Only Thiers was singled out for an atrocity. His grand house was demolished by order of the Commune. It is said he wept with rage.

Nathalie Lemel collared Arthur Rimbaud and made him wash up for an hour a day. He had a big appetite and seemed only to want to play with the kids.

"How old are you?" She asked him.

"Twelve," said Arthur Rimbaud.

"You're about as twelve as I am," she said. "You look big enough to carry a gun to me."

It startled Rimbaud out of his reverie. Shells were beginning to reach the boulevards around the Arc de Triomphe. The kids had taken him to see them fall. Wounded Federals, some on crutches with grey faces, ate in the *Le Marmite* café. At night he read to the Lost Children from his poem The Drunken Boat. He improvised spontaneous poems for them. He didn't want to grow up.

Monelle sat beside him on his matrass one night when the kids were all asleep.

"What happened to you has happened to both me and L'Oursin," she said. Then,

"You can't let it drive you crazy."

Arthur said nothing.

"Write one of your poems about it. Whenever I sing, I sing about it in a way. Go back to Charleville, Arthur."

She put her arms round him, kissed him fiercely on the lips and was gone. That night Rimbaud wrote this:

Tortured Heart

My poor heart drools at the poop

My heart is full of caporal

Spurting gobs of soup

My poor heart drools at the poop

Jeering from the troop

My poor heart drools at the poop

My heart is full of caporal.

Ithyphallic and soldierly

Insults have depraved my heart

At vespers painting frescos fresh

Ithyphallic and soldierly

O abracadabratic waves

Make my heart hurt less!

Ithyphallic and soldierly

Insults have depraved my heart.

When they've shot their wads

What shall we do my stolen heart?

Bacchic songs and Bacchic nods

When they've shot their wads

I'll have to heave my guts

My stolen heart all gobbled up

When they've shot their wads

What shall we do my stolen heart? [17]

In the morning he said goodbye to the lost children and started walking east.

Chapter Thirteen

Belle Époque

In the early summer of 1875 Auguste Renoir sat beside the dance floor of the Moulin de la Galette and painted the scene. It was a Sunday in the last week of May, four years exactly after the Commune was crushed in the Bloody Week of May 1871. In the foreground of the picture are two women talking to some men at a table drinking absinthe. The women, in beautiful clothes, look to us like bourgeois women but they are seamstresses, the same village women who had danced there five years previously. The woman standing, leaning over the girl in blue and white, fought on the barricades in a red petticoat, with clogs on her feet and a mob cap on her head. She fought with a Chassepot rifle and finally with a sword, until she was shot in the chest. The bullet just missed the top of her lung and grazed her shoulder-blade before exiting her upper back. She showed signs of life when the Versailles soldiers tried to throw her into a mass grave not far from the place where she now stands. By this time they had grown sick of the slaughter. The city stank of unburied dead and no one had the heart to shoot her. She survived. In those days a bullet made a more precise hole than bullets do now and this one missed vital organs and arteries.

In the far distance of the picture, under the biggest cluster of lights, you can just see Monelle on the bandstand in red and the glint of L'Oursin's saxophone. She is singing *Le Temps des Cerises,* the song of the Commune, love and death. About a dozen of those in the crowd under the tamarisk trees fought on the barricades. The men are bohemian small owners, republican or Jacobin in temperament, the class that was the backbone of the Central Committees. None of the *Haute Bourgeoisie* of the boulevards would have hazarded to venture into Montmartre. What Renoir painted was the dispossessed celebrating their strength and endurance while shouldering the dead weight of a parasitic, murderous class again. The Belle Époque was their gift. Everything that rises comes from below.

I heard some kind of rapid bugle call whose brazen notes sent a chill through my heart. That call was like an echo of the May days of 1871. Do they still lead soldiers against the people?

See the grains of sand and the piled-up hay and in the highest heavens the crowded stars. Where all that is seen is where we are going. And here comes the great harvest, grown in the blood of our hearts. The heads of wheat will be heavier because of that, and the harvest will be greater. See this red dew on the earth. It is blood. The grass over the dead grows higher and greener. On this earth, the charnel house of the peoples' dreams, the grass ought to grow thickly. Oh my beloved dead! The dream emerges from the scents of spring. [18]

Monelle sang of love, death and defiance while Renoir, with the sun in his heart, painted the harvest; while the dancers found strength to dance after a week of sixteen hour days. They were wearing the clothes that co-created this painting which was made by an artist who once painted pottery in a factory. The tamarisk trees grow greener for the blood of the fallen. The strengthless dead light up the coats of the drinkers with sun-dapples, or shadow the dance floor with lilac shadows. They are present. They are undefeated.

"When I sing of cherry blossom time

The blackbird sings

And lovers will have the sun in their hearts.

Blossoms fall like blood among the leaves

And in my heart a wound opens."

The old perfumer lay in the mass grave behind the windmill. When the Versailles forces approached the Buttes she barred their way with a sword in her hand. They shot her down. The circus was spared. Circus is always from another plane; perhaps inviolable. The older of the lost children were bayoneted to death in the street outside their house. The returning *Haute Bourgeoisie* of the boulevards were complaining of the noise of the firing squads. The younger children left no record. Dip and M. Verdier were still running the press and met the assault on their street from the door of the shop with guns in their hands. Nathalie Lemel was captured in the *Le Marmite* café, defiant and contemptuous. She was sent into exile in New Caledonia with Louise Michel and lived on into the twenties of the next century. Her partner in the cooperative, another bookbinder, Eugène Varlin was captured on the Buttes. He was tortured, his eyes were put out and then he was shot. He lies in the same grave as the perfumer. The soldiers of property and order slaughtered thirty five thousand people, nearly all working class, under direct orders from Adolph Thiers who became the first president of the Third Republic which governed France until 1940. General MacMohan, Duke of Magenta, who became the Republic's second president, had to drive his men to the slaughter. Eventually they refused to obey orders and the danger of disease from the unburied corpses was so great a halt was called. All the while the blackbirds sang, the cherries blossomed, the sun shone, until the last day when the rain came.

Louise Michel was fighting in the last stand in the cemetery of Montmartre when Jarowslaw Dombrowski, the commander of communard forces rode up,

"It's over," he said.

"Never!" Shouted Michel over the roar of the grapeshot.

They clasped hands in the open under fire and laughed. He was dead within half an hour. She fought on until she was the last of her companions left alive. A cannon ball tore through the cherry tree above her and showered her with broken branches and blossom. She had run out of ammunition. She put the Remington aside. She gathered the blossoms and walked under heavy fire among the shattered stones and broken angels, laying the flowers on the graves of the unruly women of Montmartre, the school mistresses and seamstresses. As always nothing touched her. She then walked calmly towards the Versailles soldiers, holding aloft the last sprig of blossom. She silenced the guns.

Notes

1. P. 12   Louise Michel recalls in her memoirs feeding milk to bats as a child. It is entirely possible to feed bats like this.

2. P. 35.   Rimbaud, from "Illuminations." Sorrell, *Arthur Rimbaud, Collected Poems,* Oxford.

3. P. 37.   Rimbaud, from "A Season in Hell." Sorrell.

4. P. 37.   Rimbaud, from "Illuminations." Sorrell.

5. P. 40   My translation.

6. P. 41   Rimbaud, from "Illuminations." Sorrell.

7. P. 41   Rimbaud, from "Illuminations." Sorrell.

8. P. 55   Louise Michel, "Memoirs." Lowry, Gunter, *The Red Virgin, Memoirs of Louise Michel,* The University of Alabama Press, 1981.

9. P. 60   Carolyn Eichner, *Surmounting the Barricades: Women in the Paris Commune,* Indiana University Press, 2004, p. 137.

10. P. 60   Eichner, p. 132.

11. P. 102   Much of the preceding narrative attributed to Michel has been quoted from Michel's Memoirs.

12. P. 110   Rimbaud, "Illuminations." Sorrell.

13. P. 198   This letter was actually written to someone other than Rigault. Quoted from Edith Thomas, *Louise Michel,* Black Rose Books 1980, Trans. Penelope Williams, P. 84.

14. P 202   Lowry, Gunter, *Memoirs,* Pp.65-66.

15. P 205   *The Commune, Paris 1871,* ed. Andrew Zonneveld, On Our Own Authority! Publishing, Atlanta, 2013.

16. P. 213   Rimbaud, from "Illuminations." Sorrell

17. P. 223. My translation.

18. P. 225. Michel, *Memoirs,* Lowry, Gunter.